SHAKUNTALA

KALIDASA

PEACOCK BOOKS

Published by
PEACOCK BOOKS
7/22, Ansari Road, Darya Ganj, New Delhi-110002
Phones : +91-11-40775252, 40775214, 23273880, 23275880
Fax : +91-11-23285873
Web : www.atlanticbooks.com
E-mail : orders@atlanticbooks.com

Peacock Books is an imprint of
Atlantic Publishers and Distributors (P) Ltd

First Published 1893

Printed & bound in India by Atlantic Print Services

Kalidasa, believed to have lived in the 4th or 5th century CE, is regarded as one of the foremost figures in classical Sanskrit literature, often referred to as the Shakespeare of India. Although little is known about his life, his profound understanding of human nature, nature, and the divine shines through in his works, which reflect the artistic flourishing of the Gupta period. His repertoire includes epic poems, plays, and lyrical verses that explore themes of love, fate, and transformation. The renowned play *Shakuntala* depicts a timeless narrative of love and separation, influencing numerous adaptations worldwide.

Noteworthy works by Kalidasa:

- *Meghaduta*
- *Kumarasambhava*
- *Malavikagnimitra*
- *Raghuvamsa*

CONTENTS

INTRODUCTION

Kalidasa— His Life and Writings

I

Kalidasa probably lived in the fifth century of the Christian era. This date, approximate as it is, must yet be given with considerable hesitation, and is by no means certain. No truly biographical data are preserved about the author, who nevertheless enjoyed a great popularity during his life, and whom the Hindus have ever regarded as the greatest of Sanskrit poets. We are thus confronted with one of the remarkable problems of literary history. For our ignorance is not due to neglect of Kalidasa's writings on the part of his countrymen, but to their strange blindness in regard to the interest and importance of historic fact. No European nation can compare with India in critical devotion to its own literature. During a period to be reckoned not by centuries but by millenniums, there has been in India an unbroken line of savants unselfishly dedicated to the perpetuation and exegesis of the native masterpieces. Editions, recensions, commentaries abound; poets have sought the exact phrase of appreciation for their predecessors: yet when we seek to reconstruct the life of their greatest poet, we have no materials except certain tantalising legends, and such data as we can gather from the writings of a man who hardly mentions himself.

One of these legends deserves to be recounted for its intrinsic interest, although it contains, so far as we can see, no grain of historic truth, and although it places Kalidasa in Benares, five hundred miles distant from the only city in which we certainly know that he spent a part of his life. According to this account, Kalidasa was a Brahman's child. At the age of six months he was left an orphan and was adopted by an ox-driver. He grew to manhood without formal education, yet with remarkable beauty and grace of manner. Now it happened that the Princess of Benares was a blue-stocking, who rejected one suitor after another, among them her father's counsellor, because they failed to reach her standard as scholars and poets. The rejected counsellor planned a cruel revenge. He took the handsome ox-driver from the street, gave him the garments of a savant and a retinue of learned doctors, then introduced him to the princess, after warning him that he was under no circumstances to open his lips. The princess was struck with his beauty and smitten to the depths of her pedantic soul by his obstinate silence, which seemed to her, as indeed it was, an evidence of profound wisdom. She desired to marry Kalidasa, and together they went to the temple. But no sooner was the ceremony performed than Kalidasa perceived an image of a bull. His early training was too much for him; the secret came out, and the bride was furious. But she relented in response to Kalidasa's entreaties, and advised him to pray for learning and poetry to the goddess Kali. The prayer was granted; education and poetical power descended miraculously to dwell with the young ox-driver, who in gratitude assumed the name Kalidasa, servant of Kali. Feeling that he owed this happy change in his very nature to his princess, he swore that he would ever treat her as his teacher, with profound respect but without familiarity. This was more than the lady had bargained for; her anger burst forth anew, and she cursed Kalidasa to meet his death at the hands of a woman. At a later date, the story continues, this curse was fulfilled. A certain king had written a half-stanza of verse, and had offered a large reward to any poet who could worthily complete it. Kalidasa completed the stanza without difficulty; but a woman whom he loved discovered his lines, and greedy of the reward herself, killed him.

Another legend represents Kalidasa as engaging in a pilgrimage to a shrine of Vishnu in Southern India, in company with two other famous writers, Bhavabhuti and Dandin. Yet another pictures Bhavabhuti as a contemporary of Kalidasa, and jealous of the less austere poet's reputation. These stories must be untrue, for it is certain that the three authors were not contemporary, yet they show a true instinct in the belief that genius seeks genius, and is rarely isolated.

This instinctive belief has been at work with the stories which connect Kalidasa with King Vikramaditya and the literary figures of his court. It has doubtless enlarged, perhaps partly falsified the facts; yet we cannot doubt that there is truth in this tradition, late though it be, and impossible though it may ever be to separate the actual from the fanciful. Here then we are on firmer ground.

King Vikramaditya ruled in the city of Ujjain, in West-central India. He was mighty both in war and in peace, winning especial glory by a decisive victory over the barbarians who pressed into India through the northern passes. Though it has not proved possible to identify this monarch with any of the known rulers, there can be no doubt that he existed and had the character attributed to him. The name Vikramaditya—Sun of Valour—is probably not a proper name, but a title like Pharaoh or Tsar. No doubt Kalidasa intended to pay a tribute to his patron, the Sun of Valour, in the very title of his play, *Urvashi won by Valour*.

King Vikramaditya was a great patron of learning and of poetry. Ujjain during his reign was the most brilliant capital in the world, nor has it to this day lost all the lustre shed upon it by that splendid court. Among the eminent men gathered there, nine were particularly distinguished, and these nine are known as the "nine gems." Some of the nine gems were poets, others represented science—astronomy, medicine, lexicography. It is quite true that the details of this late tradition concerning the nine gems are open to suspicion, yet the central fact is not doubtful: that there was at this time and place a great quickening of the human mind, an artistic impulse creating works that cannot perish. Ujjain in the days of Vikramaditya stands worthily beside Athens, Rome, Florence, and London in their great centuries. Here is the substantial fact behind Max Muumlller's often ridiculed theory of the renaissance of Sanskrit literature. It is quite false to suppose, as some appear to do, that this theory has been invalidated by the discovery of certain literary products which antedate Kalidasa. It might even be said that those rare and happy centuries that see a man as great as Homer or Vergil or Kalidasa or Shakespeare partake in that one man of a renaissance.

It is interesting to observe that the centuries of intellectual darkness in Europe have sometimes coincided with centuries of light in India. The Vedas were composed for the most part before Homer; Kalidasa and his contemporaries lived while Rome was tottering under barbarian assault.

To the scanty and uncertain data of late traditions may be added some information about Kalidasa's life gathered from his own writings. He mentions his own name only in the prologues to his three plays, and here with a modesty that is charming indeed, yet tantalising. One wishes for a portion of the communicativeness that characterises some of the Indian poets. He speaks in the first person only once, in the verses introductory to his epic poem *The Dynasty of Raghu*.Here also we feel his modesty, and here once more we are balked of details as to his life.

We know from Kalidasa's writings that he spent at least a part of his life in the city of Ujjain. He refers to Ujjain more than once, and in a manner hardly possible to one who did not know and love the city. Especially in his poem *The Cloud-Messenger* does he dwell upon the city's charms, and even bids the cloud make a détour in his long journey lest he should miss making its acquaintance.

We learn further that Kalidasa travelled widely in India. The fourth canto of *The Dynasty of Raghu* describes a tour about the whole of India and even into regions which are beyond the borders of a narrowly measured India. It is hard to believe that Kalidasa had not himself made such a "grand tour"; so much of truth there may be in the tradition which sends him on a pilgrimage to Southern India. The thirteenth canto of the same epic and *The Cloud-Messenger* also describe long journeys over India, for the most part through regions far from Ujjain. It is the mountains which impress him most deeply. His works are full of the Himalayas. Apart from his earliest drama and the slight poem called *The Seasons*, there is not one of them which is not fairly redolent of mountains. One, *The Birth of the War-god*, might be said to be all mountains. Nor was it only Himalayan grandeur and sublimity which attracted him; for, as a Hindu critic has acutely observed, he is the only Sanskrit poet who has described a certain flower that grows in Kashmir. The sea interested him less. To him, as to most Hindus, the ocean was a beautiful, terrible barrier, not a highway to adventure. The "sea-belted earth" of which Kalidasa speaks means to him the mainland of India.

Another conclusion that may be certainly drawn from Kalidasa's writing is this, that he was a man of sound and rather extensive education. He was not indeed a prodigy of learning, like Bhavabhuti in his own country or Milton in England, yet no man could write as he did without hard and intelligent study. To begin with, he had a minutely accurate knowledge of the Sanskrit language, at a time when Sanskrit was to some extent an artificial tongue. Somewhat too much stress is often laid upon this point, as if the writers of the classical period in India were composing in a foreign language. Every writer, especially every poet, composing in any language, writes in what may be called a strange idiom; that is, he does not write as he talks. Yet it is true that the gap between written language and vernacular was wider in Kalidasa's day than it has often been. The Hindus themselves regard twelve years' study as requisite for the mastery of the "chief of all sciences, the science of grammar." That Kalidasa had mastered this science his works bear abundant witness.

He likewise mastered the works on rhetoric and dramatic theory—subjects which Hindu savants have treated with great, if sometimes hair-splitting, ingenuity. The profound and subtle systems of philosophy were also possessed by Kalidasa, and he had some knowledge of astronomy and law.

But it was not only in written books that Kalidasa was deeply read. Rarely has a man walked our earth who observed the phenomena of living nature as accurately as he, though his accuracy was of course that of the poet, not that of the scientist. Much is lost to us who grow up among other animals and plants; yet we can appreciate his "bee-black hair," his ashoka-tree that "sheds his blossoms in a rain of tears," his river wearing a sombre veil of mist:

Although her reeds seem hands that clutch the dressTo hide her charms;

his picture of the day-blooming water-lily at sunset:

The water-lily closes, butWith wonderful reluctancy;As if it troubled her to shutHer door of welcome to the bee.

The religion of any great poet is always a matter of interest, especially the religion of a Hindu poet; for the Hindus have ever been a deeply and creatively religious people. So far as we can judge, Kalidasa moved among the jarring sects with sympathy for all, fanaticism for none. The dedicatory prayers that introduce his dramas are addressed to Shiva. This is hardly more than a convention, for Shiva is the patron of literature. If one of his epics, *The Birth of the War-god*, is distinctively Shivaistic, the other, *The Dynasty of Raghu*, is no less Vishnuite in tendency. If the hymn to Vishnu in *The Dynasty of Raghu* is an expression of Vedantic monism, the hymn to Brahma in *The Birth of the War-god* gives equally clear expression to the rival dualism of the Sankhya system. Nor are the Yoga doctrine and Buddhism left without sympathetic mention. We are therefore justified in concluding that Kalidasa was, in matters of religion, what William James would call "healthy-minded," emphatically not a "sick soul."

There are certain other impressions of Kalidasa's life and personality which gradually become convictions in the mind of one who reads and re-reads his poetry, though they are less easily susceptible of exact proof. One feels certain that he was physically handsome, and the handsome Hindu is a wonderfully fine type of manhood. One knows that he possessed a fascination for women, as they in turn fascinated him. One knows that children loved him. One becomes convinced that he never suffered any morbid, soul-shaking experience such as besetting religious doubt brings with it, or the pangs of despised love; that on the contrary he moved among men and women with a serene and godlike tread, neither self-indulgent nor ascetic, with mind and senses ever alert to every form of beauty. We know that his poetry was popular while he lived, and we cannot doubt that his personality was equally attractive, though it is probable that no contemporary knew the full measure of his greatness. For his nature was one of singular balance, equally at home in a splendid court and on a lonely mountain, with men of high and of low degree. Such men are never fully appreciated during life. They continue to grow after they are dead.

II

Kalidasa left seven works which have come down to us: three dramas, two epics, one elegiac poem, and one descriptive poem. Many other works, including even an astronomical treatise, have been attributed to him; they are certainly not his. Perhaps there was more than one author who bore the name Kalidasa; perhaps certain later writers were more concerned for their work than for personal fame. On the other hand, there is no reason to doubt that the seven recognised works are in truth from Kalidasa's hand. The only one concerning which there is reasonable room for suspicion is the short poem descriptive of the seasons, and this is fortunately the least important of the seven. Nor is there evidence to show that any considerable poem has been lost, unless it be true that the concluding cantos of one of the epics have perished. We are thus in a fortunate position in reading Kalidasa: we have substantially all that he wrote, and run no risk of ascribing to him any considerable work from another hand.

Of these seven works, four are poetry throughout; the three dramas, like all Sanskrit dramas, are written in prose, with a generous mingling of lyric and descriptive stanzas. The poetry, even in the epics, is stanzaic; no part of it can fairly be compared to English blank verse. Classical Sanskrit verse, so far as structure is concerned, has much in common with familiar Greek and Latin forms: it makes no systematic use of rhyme; it depends for its rhythm not upon accent, but upon quantity. The natural medium of translation into English seems to me to be the rhymed stanza in the present work the rhymed stanza has been used, with a consistency perhaps too rigid, wherever the original is in verse.

Kalidasa's three dramas bear the names: *Malavika and Agnimitra*, *Urvashi*, and *Shakuntala*. The two epics are *The Dynasty of Raghu* and *The Birth of the War-god*. The elegiac poem is called *The Cloud-Messenger*, and the descriptive poem is entitled *The Seasons*. It may be well to state briefly the more salient features of the Sanskrit *genres* to which these works belong.

The drama proved in India, as in other countries, a congenial form to many of the most eminent poets. The Indian drama has a marked individuality, but stands nearer to the modern European theatre than to that of ancient Greece; for the plays, with a very few exceptions, have no religious significance, and deal with love between man and woman. Although tragic elements may be present, a tragic ending is forbidden. Indeed, nothing regarded as disagreeable, such as fighting or even kissing, is permitted on the stage; here Europe may perhaps learn a lesson in taste. Stage properties were few and simple, while particular care was lavished on the music. The female parts were played by women. The plays very rarely have long monologues, even the inevitable prologue being divided between two speakers, but a Hindu audience was tolerant of lyrical digression.

It may be said, though the statement needs qualification in both directions, that the Indian dramas have less action and less individuality in the characters, but more poetical charm than the dramas of modern Europe.

On the whole, Kalidasa was remarkably faithful to the ingenious but somewhat over-elaborate conventions of Indian dramaturgy. His first play, the *Malavika and Agnimitra*, is entirely conventional in plot. The *Shakuntala* is transfigured by the character of the heroine. The *Urvashi*, in spite of detail beauty, marks a distinct decline.

The Dynasty of Raghu and *The Birth of the War-god* belong to a species of composition which it is not easy to name accurately. The Hindu name *kavya* has been rendered by artificial epic, *épopée savante, Kunstgedicht*. It is best perhaps to use the term epic, and to qualify the term by explanation.

The *kavyas* differ widely from the *Mahabharata* and the *Ramayana*, epics which resemble the *Iliad* and *Odyssey* less in outward form than in their character as truly national poems. The *kavya* is a narrative poem written in a sophisticated age by a learned poet, who possesses all the resources of an elaborate rhetoric and metric. The subject is drawn from time-honoured mythology. The poem is divided into cantos, written not in blank verse but in stanzas. Several stanza-forms are commonly employed in the same poem, though not in the same canto, except that the concluding verses of a canto are not infrequently written in a metre of more compass than the remainder.

I have called *The Cloud-Messenger* an elegiac poem, though it would not perhaps meet the test of a rigid definition. The Hindus class it with *The Dynasty of Raghu* and *The Birth of the War-god* as a *kavya*, but this classification simply evidences their embarrassment. In fact, Kalidasa created in *The Cloud-Messenger* a new *genre*. No further explanation is needed here, as the entire poem is translated below.

The short descriptive poem called *The Seasons* has abundant analogues in other literatures, and requires no comment.

It is not possible to fix the chronology of Kalidasa's writings, yet we are not wholly in the dark. *Malavika and Agnimitra* was certainly his first drama, almost certainly his first work. It is a reasonable conjecture, though nothing more, that Urvashi was written late, when the poet's powers were waning. The introductory stanzas of *The Dynasty of Raghu* suggest that this epic was written before *The Birth of the War-god*, though the inference is far from certain. Again, it is reasonable to assume that the great works on which Kalidasa's fame chiefly rests—*Shakuntala*, *The Cloud-Messenger*, *The Dynasty of Raghu*, the first eight cantos of *The Birth of the War-god*—were composed when he was in the prime of manhood. But as to the succession of these four works we can do little but guess.

Kalidasa's glory depends primarily upon the quality of his work, yet would be much diminished if he had failed in bulk and variety. In India, more than would be the case in Europe, the extent of his writing is an indication of originality and power; for the poets of the classical period underwent an education that encouraged an exaggerated fastidiousness, and they wrote for a public meticulously critical. Thus the great Bhavabhuti spent his life in constructing three dramas; mighty spirit though he was, he yet suffers from the very scrupulosity of his labour. In this matter, as in others, Kalidasa preserves his intellectual balance and his spiritual initiative: what greatness of soul is required for this, every one knows who has ever had the misfortune to differ in opinion from an intellectual clique.

III

Le nom de Kâlidâsa domine la poésie indienne et la résume brillamment. Le drame, l'épopée savante, l'élégie attestent aujourd'hui encore la puissance et la souplesse de ce magnifique génie; seul entre les disciples de Sarasvatî [the goddess of eloquence], il a eu le bonheur de produire un chef-d'œuvre vraiment classique, où l'Inde s'admire et où l'humanité se reconnaît. Les applaudissements qui saluèrent la naissance de Çakuntalâ à Ujjayinî ont après de longs siècles éclaté d'un bout du monde à l'autre, quand William Jones l'eut révélée à l'Occident. Kâlidâsa a marqué sa place dans cette pléiade étincelante où chaque nom résume une période de l'esprit humain. La série de ces noms forme l'histoire, ou plutôt elle est l'histoire même.

It is hardly possible to say anything true about Kalidasa's achievement which is not already contained in this appreciation. Yet one loves to expand the praise, even though realising that the critic is by his very nature a fool. Here there shall at any rate be none of that cold-blooded criticism which imagines itself set above a world-author to appraise and judge, but a generous tribute of affectionate admiration.

The best proof of a poet's greatness is the inability of men to live without him; in other words, his power to win and hold through centuries the love and admiration of his own people, especially when that people has shown itself capable of high intellectual and spiritual achievement.

For something like fifteen hundred years, Kalidasa has been more widely read in India than any other author who wrote in Sanskrit. There have also been many attempts to express in words the secret of his abiding power: such attempts can never be wholly successful, yet they are not without considerable interest. Thus Bana, a celebrated novelist of the seventh century, has the following lines in some stanzas of poetical criticism which he prefixes to a historical romance:

Where find a soul that does not thrillIn Kalidasa's verse to meetThe smooth, inevitable linesLike blossom-clusters, honey-sweet?

A later writer, speaking of Kalidasa and another poet, is more laconic in this alliterative line: *Bhaso hasah, Kalidaso vilasah*—Bhasa is mirth, Kalidasa is grace.

These two critics see Kalidasa's grace, his sweetness, his delicate taste, without doing justice to the massive quality without which his poetry could not have survived.

Though Kalidasa has not been as widely appreciated in Europe as he deserves, he is the only Sanskrit poet who can properly be said to have been appreciated at all. Here he must struggle with the truly Himalayan barrier of language. Since there will never be many Europeans, even among the cultivated, who will find it possible to study the intricate Sanskrit language, there remains only one means of presentation. None knows the cruel inadequacy of poetical translation like the translator. He understands better than others can, the significance of the position which Kalidasa has won in Europe. When Sir William Jones first translated the *Shakuntala* in 1789, his work was enthusiastically received in Europe, and most warmly, as was fitting, by the greatest living poet of Europe. Since that day, as is testified by new translations and by reprints of the old, there have been many thousands who have read at least one of Kalidasa's works; other thousands have seen it on the stage in Europe and America.

How explain a reputation that maintains itself indefinitely and that conquers a new continent after a lapse of thirteen hundred years? None can explain it, yet certain contributory causes can be named.

No other poet in any land has sung of happy love between man and woman as Kalidasa sang. Every one of his works is a love-poem, however much more it may be. Yet the theme is so infinitely varied that the reader never wearies. If one were to doubt from a study of European literature, comparing the ancient classics with modern works, whether romantic love be the expression of a natural instinct, be not rather a morbid survival of decaying chivalry, he has only to turn to India's independently growing literature to find the question settled. Kalidasa's love-poetry rings as true in our ears as it did in his countrymen's ears fifteen hundred years ago.

It is of love eventually happy, though often struggling for a time against external obstacles, that Kalidasa writes. There is nowhere in his works a trace of that not quite healthy feeling that sometimes assumes the name "modern love." If it were not so, his poetry could hardly have survived; for happy love, blessed with children, is surely the more fundamental thing. In his drama *Urvashi* he is ready to change and greatly injure a tragic story, given him by long tradition, in order that a loving pair may not be permanently separated. One apparent exception there is—the story of Rama and Sita in *The Dynasty of Raghu*. In this case it must be remembered that Rama is an incarnation of Vishnu, and the story of a mighty god incarnate is not to be lightly tampered with.

It is perhaps an inevitable consequence of Kalidasa's subject that his women appeal more strongly to a modern reader than his men. The man is the more variable phenomenon, and though manly virtues are the same in all countries and centuries, the emphasis has been variously laid. But the true woman seems timeless, universal. I know of no poet, unless it be Shakespeare, who has given the world a group of heroines so individual yet so universal; heroines as true, as tender, as brave as are Indumati, Sita, Parvati, the Yaksha's bride, and Shakuntala.

Kalidasa could not understand women without understanding children. It would be difficult to find anywhere lovelier pictures of childhood than those in which our poet presents the little Bharata, Ayus, Raghu, Kumara. It is a fact worth noticing that Kalidasa's children are all boys. Beautiful as his women are, he never does more than glance at a little girl.

Another pervading note of Kalidasa's writing is his love of external nature. No doubt it is easier for a Hindu, with his almost instinctive belief in reincarnation, to feel that all life, from plant to god, is truly one; yet none, even among the Hindus, has expressed this feeling with such convincing beauty as has Kalidasa. It is hardly true to say that he personifies rivers and mountains and trees; to him they have a conscious individuality as truly and as certainly as animals or men or gods. Fully to appreciate Kalidasa's poetry one must have spent some weeks at least among wild mountains and forests untouched by man; there the conviction grows that trees and flowers are indeed individuals, fully conscious of a personal life and happy in that life. The return to urban surroundings makes the vision fade; yet the memory remains, like a great love or a glimpse of mystic insight, as an intuitive conviction of a higher truth.

Kalidasa's knowledge of nature is not only sympathetic, it is also minutely accurate. Not only are the snows and windy music of the Himalayas, the mighty current of the sacred Ganges, his possession; his too are smaller streams and trees and every littlest flower. It is delightful to imagine a meeting between Kalidasa and Darwin. They would have understood each other perfectly; for in each the same kind of imagination worked with the same wealth of observed fact.

I have already hinted at the wonderful balance in Kalidasa's character, by virtue of which he found himself equally at home in a palace and in a wilderness. I know not with whom to compare him in this; even Shakespeare, for all his magical insight into natural beauty, is primarily a poet of the human heart. That can hardly be said of Kalidasa, nor can it be said that he is primarily a poet of natural beauty. The two characters unite in him, it might almost be said, chemically. The matter which I am clumsily endeavouring to make plain is beautifully epitomised in *The Cloud-Messenger*. The former half is a description of external nature, yet interwoven with human feeling; the latter half is a picture of a human heart, yet the picture is framed in natural beauty. So exquisitely is the thing done that none can say which half is superior. Of those who read this perfect poem in the original text, some are more moved by the one, some by the other. Kalidasa understood in the fifth century what Europe did not learn until the nineteenth, and even now comprehends only imperfectly: that the world was not made for man, that man reaches his full stature only as he realises the dignity and worth of life that is not human.

That Kalidasa seized this truth is a magnificent tribute to his intellectual power, a quality quite as necessary to great poetry as perfection of form. Poetical fluency is not rare; intellectual grasp is not very uncommon: but the combination has not been found perhaps more than a dozen times since the world began. Because he possessed this harmonious combination, Kalidasa ranks not with Anacreon and Horace and Shelley, but with Sophocles, Vergil, Milton.

He would doubtless have been somewhat bewildered by Wordsworth's gospel of nature. "The world is too much with us," we can fancy him repeating. "How can the world, the beautiful human world, be too much with us? How can sympathy with one form of life do other than vivify our sympathy with other forms of life?"

It remains to say what can be said in a foreign language of Kalidasa's style. We have seen that he had a formal and systematic education; in this respect he is rather to be compared with Milton and Tennyson than with Shakespeare or Burns. He was completely master of his learning. In an age and a country which reprobated carelessness but were tolerant of pedantry, he held the scales with a wonderfully even hand, never heedless and never indulging in the elaborate trifling with Sanskrit diction which repels the reader from much of Indian literature. It is true that some western critics have spoken of his disfiguring conceits and puerile plays on words. One can only wonder whether these critics have ever read Elizabethan literature; for Kalidasa's style is far less obnoxious to such condemnation than Shakespeare's. That he had a rich and glowing imagination, "excelling in metaphor," as the Hindus themselves affirm, is indeed true; that he may, both in youth and age, have written lines which would not have passed his scrutiny in the vigour of manhood, it is not worth while to deny: yet the total effect left by his poetry is one of extraordinary sureness and delicacy of taste. This is scarcely a matter for argument; a reader can do no more than state his own subjective impression, though he is glad to find that impression confirmed by the unanimous authority of fifty generations of Hindus, surely the most competent judges on such a point.

Analysis of Kalidasa's writings might easily be continued, but analysis can never explain life. The only real criticism is subjective. We know that Kalidasa is a very great poet, because the world has not been able to leave him alone.

ARTHUR W. RYDER

A PLAY IN SEVEN ACTS

Dramatis Personæ

KING DUSHYANTA.	
BHARATA,	*nicknamed* All-tamer, *his son.*
MADHAVYA,	*a clown, his companion.*
His charioteer.	
RAIVATAKA,	*a door-keeper.*
BHADRASENA,	*a general.*
KARABHAKA,	*a servant.*
PARVATAYANA,	*a chamberlain.*
SOMARATA,	*a chaplain.*
KANVA,	*hermit-father.*
SHARNGARAVA SHARADVATA HARITA	} *his pupils.*
DURVASAS,	*an irascible sage.*
The chief of police.	
SUCHAKA JANUKA	} *policemen.*
A fisherman.	
SHAKUNTALA,	*foster-child of Kanva.*

ANUSUYA PRIYAMVADA	} *her friends.*
GAUTAMI,	*hermit-mother.*
KASHYAPA,	*father of the gods.*
ADITI,	*mother of the gods.*
MATALI,	*charioteer of heaven's king.*
GALAVA,	*a pupil in heaven.*
MISHRAKESHI,	*a heavenly nymph.*

Stage-director and actress (in the prologue), hermits and hermit-women, two court poets, palace attendants, invisible fairies.

The first four acts pass in Kanva's forest hermitage; acts five and six in the king's palace; act seven on a heavenly mountain. The time is perhaps seven years.

PROLOGUE

BENEDICTION UPON AUDIENCE

Eight forms has Shiva, lord of all and king:
And these are water, first created thing;
And fire, which speeds the sacrifice begun;
The priest; and time's dividers, moon and sun;
The all-embracing ether, path of sound;
The earth, wherein all seeds of life are found;
And air, the breath of life: may he draw near,
Revealed in these, and bless those gathered here.

The stage-director. Enough of this! (*Turning toward the dressing-room.*) Madam, if you are ready, pray come here. (*Enter an actress.*)

Actress. Here I am, sir. What am I to do?

Director. Our audience is very discriminating, and we are to offer them a new play, called *Shakuntala and the ring of recognition*, written by the famous Kalidasa. Every member of the cast must be on his mettle.

Actress. Your arrangements are perfect. Nothing will go wrong.

Director (*smiling*). To tell the truth, madam,

Until the wise are satisfied,
I cannot feel that skill is shown;
The best-trained mind requires support,
And does not trust itself alone.

Actress. True. What shall we do first?

Director. First, you must sing something to please the ears of the audience.

Actress. What season of the year shall I sing about?

Director. Why, sing about the pleasant summer which has just begun. For at this time of year

A mid-day plunge will temper heat;
The breeze is rich with forest flowers;
To slumber in the shade is sweet;
And charming are the twilight hours.

Actress (*sings*).

The siris-blossoms fair,
With pollen laden,
Are plucked to deck her hair
By many a maiden,
But gently; flowers like these
Are kissed by eager bees.

Director. Well done! The whole theatre is captivated by your song, and sits as if painted. What play shall we give them to keep their good-will?

Actress. Why, you just told me we were to give a new play called *Shakuntala and the ring*.

Director. Thank you for reminding me. For the moment I had quite forgotten.

Your charming song had carried me away
As the deer enticed the hero of our play.

(*Exeunt ambo*.)

ACT
I
THE HUNT

(*Enter, in a chariot, pursuing a deer,* KING DUSHYANTA, *bow and arrow in hand; and a charioteer.*)

Charioteer (*Looking at the king and the deer*). Your Majesty,

I see you hunt the spotted deer
With shafts to end his race,
As though God Shiva should appear
In his immortal chase.

King. Charioteer, the deer has led us a long chase. And even now

His neck in beauty bends
As backward looks he sends
At my pursuing car
That threatens death from far.
Fear shrinks to half the body small;
See how he fears the arrow's fall!

The path he takes is strewed
With blades of grass half-chewed
From jaws wide with the stress
Of fevered weariness.
He leaps so often and so high,
He does not seem to run, but fly.

(*In surprise.*) Pursue as I may, I can hardly keep him in sight.

Charioteer. Your Majesty, I have been holding the horses back because the ground was rough. This checked us and gave the deer a lead. Now we are on level ground, and you will easily overtake him.

King. Then let the reins hang loose.

Charioteer. Yes, your Majesty. (*He counterfeits rapid motion.*) Look, your Majesty!

The lines hang loose; the steeds unreined
Dart forward with a will.
Their ears are pricked; their necks are strained;
Their plumes lie straight and still.
They leave the rising dust behind;
They seem to float upon the wind.

King (*joyfully*). See! The horses are gaining on the deer.

As onward and onward the chariot flies,
The small flashes large to my dizzy eyes.
What is cleft in twain, seems to blur and mate;
What is crooked in nature, seems to be straight.
Things at my side in an instant appear
Distant, and things in the distance, near.

A voice behind the scenes. O King, this deer belongs to the hermitage, and must not be killed.

Charioteer (*listening and looking*). Your Majesty, here are two hermits, come to save the deer at the moment when your arrow was about to fall.

King (*hastily*). Stop the chariot.

Charioteer. Yes, your Majesty. (*He does so. Enter a hermit with his pupil.*)

Hermit (*lifting his hand*). O King, this deer belongs to the hermitage.

Why should his tender form expire,
As blossoms perish in the fire?
How could that gentle life endure
The deadly arrow, sharp and sure?

Restore your arrow to the quiver;
To you were weapons lent
The broken-hearted to deliver,
Not strike the innocent.

King (*bowing low*). It is done. (*He does so.*)

Hermit (*joyfully*). A deed worthy of you, scion of Puru's race, and shining example of kings. May you beget a son to rule earth and heaven.

King (*bowing low*). I am thankful for a Brahman's blessing.

The two hermits. O King, we are on our way to gather firewood. Here, along the bank of the Malini, you may see the hermitage of Father Kanva, over which Shakuntala presides, so to speak, as guardian deity. Unless other deities prevent, pray enter here and receive a welcome. Besides,

Beholding pious hermit-rites
Preserved from fearful harm,
Perceive the profit of the scars
On your protecting arm.

King. Is the hermit father there?

The two hermits. No, he has left his daughter to welcome guests, and has just gone to Somatirtha, to avert an evil fate that threatens her.

King. Well, I will see her. She shall feel my devotion, and report it to the sage.

The two hermits. Then we will go on our way. (*Exit hermit with pupil.*)

King. Charioteer, drive on. A sight of the pious hermitage will purify us.

Charioteer. Yes, your Majesty. (*He counterfeits motion again.*)

King (*looking about*). One would know, without being told, that this is the precinct of a pious grove.

Charioteer. How so?

King. Do you not see? Why, here

Are rice-grains, dropped from bills of parrot chicks
Beneath the trees; and pounding-stones where sticks
A little almond-oil; and trustful deer
That do not run away as we draw near;
And river-paths that are besprinkled yet
From trickling hermit-garments, clean and wet.

Besides,

The roots of trees are washed by many a stream
That breezes ruffle; and the flowers' red gleam
Is dimmed by pious smoke; and fearless fawns
Move softly on the close-cropped forest lawns.

Charioteer. It is all true.

King (*after a little*). We must not disturb the hermitage. Stop here while I dismount.

Charioteer. I am holding the reins. Dismount, your Majesty.

King (*dismounts and looks at himself*). One should wear modest garments on entering a hermitage. Take these jewels and the bow. (*He gives them to the charioteer.*) Before I return from my visit to the hermits, have the horses' backs wet down.

Charioteer. Yes, your Majesty. (*Exit.*)

King (*walking and looking about*). The hermitage! Well, I will enter. (*As he does so, he feels a throbbing in his arm.*)

A tranquil spot! Why should I thrill?
Love cannot enter there—
Yet to inevitable things
Doors open everywhere.

A voice behind the scenes. This way, girls!

King (*listening*). I think I hear some one to the right of the grove. I must find out. (*He walks and looks about.*) Ah, here are hermit-girls, with watering-pots just big enough for them to handle. They are coming in this direction to water the young trees. They are charming!

The city maids, for all their pains,
Seem not so sweet and good;
Our garden blossoms yield to these
Flower-children of the wood.

I will draw back into the shade and wait for them. (*He stands, gazing toward them. Enter* SHAKUNTALA, *as described, and her two friends.*)

First friend. It seems to me, dear, that Father Kanva cares more for the hermitage trees than he does for you. You are delicate as a jasmine blossom, yet he tells you to fill the trenches about the trees.

Shakuntala. Oh, it isn't Father's bidding so much. I feel like a real sister to them. (*She waters the trees.*)

Priyamvada. Shakuntala, we have watered the trees that blossom in the summer-time. Now let's sprinkle those whose flowering-time is past. That will be a better deed, because we shall not be working for a reward.

Shakuntala. What a pretty idea! (*She does so.*)

King (*to himself*). And this is Kanva's daughter, Shakuntala. (*In surprise.*) The good Father does wrong to make her wear the hermit's dress of bark.

The sage who yokes her artless charm
With pious pain and grief,
Would try to cut the toughest vine
With a soft, blue lotus-leaf.

Well, I will step behind a tree and see how she acts with her friends. (*He conceals himself.*)

Shakuntala. Oh, Anusuya! Priyamvada has fastened this bark dress so tight that it hurts. Please loosen it. (ANUSUYA *does so.*)

Priyamvada (*laughing*). You had better blame your own budding charms for that.

King. She is quite right.

Beneath the barken dress
Upon the shoulder tied,
In maiden loveliness
Her young breast seems to hide,

As when a flower amid
The leaves by autumn tossed—
Pale, withered leaves—lies hid,
And half its grace is lost.

Yet in truth the bark dress is not an enemy to her beauty. It serves as an added ornament. For

The meanest vesture glows
On beauty that enchants:

The lotus lovelier shows
Amid dull water-plants;

The moon in added splendour
Shines for its spot of dark;
Yet more the maiden slender
Charms in her dress of bark.

Shakuntala (*looking ahead*). Oh, girls, that mango-tree is trying to tell me something with his branches that move in the wind like fingers. I must go and see him. (*She does so.*)

Priyamvada. There, Shakuntala, stand right where you are a minute.

Shakuntala. Why?

Priyamvada. When I see you there, it looks as if a vine were clinging to the mango-tree.

Shakuntala. I see why they call you the flatterer.

King. But the flattery is true.

Her arms are tender shoots; her lips
Arc blossoms red and warm;
Bewitching youth begins to flower
In beauty on her form.

Anusuya. Oh, Shakuntala! Here is the jasmine-vine that you named Light of the Grove. She has chosen the mango-tree as her husband.

Shakuntala (*approaches and looks at it, joyfully*). What a pretty pair they make. The jasmine shows her youth in her fresh flowers, and the mango-tree shows his strength in his ripening fruit. (*She stands gazing at them.*)

Priyamvada (*smiling*). Anusuya, do you know why Shakuntala looks so hard at the Light of the Grove?

Anusuya. No. Why?

Priyamvada. She is thinking how the Light of the Grove has found a good tree, and hoping that she will meet a fine lover.

Shakuntala. That's what you want for yourself. (*She tips her watering-pot.*)

Anusuya. Look, Shakuntala! Here is the spring-creeper that Father Kanva tended with his own hands—just as he did you. You are forgetting her.

Shakuntala. I'd forget myself sooner. (*She goes to the creeper and looks at it, joyfully.*) Wonderful! Wonderful! Priyamvada, I have something pleasant to tell you.

Priyamvada. What is it, dear?

Shakuntala. It is out of season, but the spring-creeper is covered with buds down to the very root.

The two friends (*running up*). Really?

Shakuntala. Of course. Can't you see?

Priyamvada (*looking at it joyfully*). And I have something pleasant to tell *you*. You are to be married soon.

Shakuntala (*snappishly*). You know that's just what you want for yourself.

Priyamvada. I'm not teasing. I really heard Father Kanva say that this flowering vine was to be a symbol of your coming happiness.

Anusuya. Priyamvada, that is why Shakuntala waters the spring-creeper so lovingly.

Shakuntala. She is my sister. Why shouldn't I give her water? (*She tips her watering-pot.*)

King. May I hope that she is the hermit's daughter by a mother of a different caste? But it *must* be so.

Surely, she may become a warrior's bride;
Else, why these longings in an honest mind?
The motions of a blameless heart decide
Of right and wrong, when reason leaves us blind.

Yet I will learn the whole truth.

Shakuntala (*excitedly*). Oh, oh! A bee has left the jasmine-vine and is flying into my face. (*She shows herself annoyed by the bee.*)

King (*ardently*).

As the bee about her flies,
Swiftly her bewitching eyes
Turn to watch his flight.
She is practising to-day
Coquetry and glances' play
Not from love, but fright.

(*Jealously.*)

Eager bee, you lightly skim
O'er the eyelid's trembling rim
Toward the cheek aquiver.
Gently buzzing round her cheek,
Whispering in her ear, you seek
Secrets to deliver.

While her hands that way and this
Strike at you, you steal a kiss,
Love's all, honeymaker.
I know nothing but her name,
Not her caste, nor whence she came—
You, my rival, take her.

Shakuntala. Oh, girls! Save me from this dreadful bee!

The two friends (*smiling*). Who are we, that we should save you? Call upon Dushyanta. For pious groves are in the protection of the king.

King. A good opportunity to present myself. Have no—(*He checks himself. Aside*.) No, they would see that I am the king. I prefer to appear as a guest.

Shakuntala. He doesn't leave me alone! I am going to run away. (*She takes a step and looks about*.) Oh, dear! Oh, dear! He is following me. Please save me.

King (*hastening forward*). Ah!

A king of Puru's mighty line
Chastises shameless churls;
What insolent is he who baits
These artless hermit-girls?

(*The girls are a little flurried on seeing the king*.)

Anusuya. It is nothing very dreadful, sir. But our friend (*indicating* SHAKUNTALA) was teased and frightened by a bee.

King (*to* SHAKUNTALA). I hope these pious days are happy ones. (SHAKUNTALA's *eyes drop in embarrassment*.)

Anusuya. Yes, now that we receive such a distinguished guest.

Priyamvada. Welcome, sir. Go to the cottage, Shakuntala, and bring fruit. This water will do to wash the feet.

King. Your courteous words are enough to make me feel at home.

Anusuya. Then, sir, pray sit down and rest on this shady bench.

King. You, too, are surely wearied by your pious task. Pray be seated a moment.

Priyamvada (*aside to* SHAKUNTALA). My dear, we must be polite to our guest. Shall we sit down? (*The three girls sit*.)

Shakuntala (*to herself*). Oh, why do I have such feelings when I see this man? They seem wrong in a hermitage.

King (*looking at the girls*). It is delightful to see your friendship. For you are all young and beautiful.

Priyamvada (*aside to* ANUSUYA). Who is he, dear? With his mystery, and his dignity, and his courtesy? He acts like a king and a gentleman.

Anusuya. I am curious too. I am going to ask him. (*Aloud.*) Sir, you are so very courteous that I make bold to ask you something. What royal family do you adorn, sir? What country is grieving at your absence? Why does a gentleman so delicately bred submit to the weary journey into our pious grove?

Shakuntala (*aside*). Be brave, my heart. Anusuya speaks your very thoughts.

King (*aside*). Shall I tell at once who I am, or conceal it? (*He reflects.*) This will do. (*Aloud.*) I am a student of Scripture. It is my duty to see justice done in the cities of the king. And I have come to this hermitage on a tour of inspection.

Anusuya. Then we of the hermitage have some one to take care of us. (SHAKUNTALA *shows embarrassment.*)

The two friends (*observing the demeanour of the pair. Aside to* SHAKUNTALA). Oh, Shakuntala! If only Father were here to-day.

Shakuntala. What would he do?

The two friends. He would make our distinguished guest happy, if it took his most precious treasure.

Shakuntala (*feigning anger*). Go away! You mean something. I'll not listen to you.

King. I too would like to ask a question about your friend.

The two friends. Sir, your request is a favour to us.

King. Father Kanva lives a lifelong hermit. Yet you say that your friend is his daughter. How can that be?

Anusuya. Listen, sir. There is a majestic royal sage named Kaushika—

King. Ah, yes. The famous Kaushika.

Anusuya. Know, then, that he is the source of our friend's being. But Father Kanva is her real father, because he took care of her when she was abandoned.

King. You waken my curiosity with the word "abandoned." May I hear the whole story?

Anusuya. Listen, sir. Many years ago, that royal sage was leading a life of stern austerities, and the gods, becoming strangely jealous, sent the nymph Menaka to disturb his devotions.

King. Yes, the gods feel this jealousy toward the austerities of others. And then—

Anusuya. Then in the lovely spring-time he saw her intoxicating beauty—(*She stops in embarrassment.*)

King. The rest is plain. Surely, she is the daughter of the nymph.

Anusuya. Yes.

King. It is as it should be.

To beauty such as this
No woman could give birth;
The quivering lightning flash
Is not a child of earth.

(SHAKUNTALA *hangs her head in confusion.*) *King* (*to himself*). Ah, my wishes become hopes.

Priyamvada (*looking with a smile at* SHAKUNTALA). Sir, it seems as if you had more to say. (SHAKUNTALA *threatens her friend with her finger.*)

King. You are right. Your pious life interests me, and I have another question.

Priyamvada. Do not hesitate. We hermit people stand ready to answer all demands.

King. My question is this:

Does she, till marriage only, keep her vow
As hermit-maid, that shames the ways of love?

Or must her soft eyes ever see, as now,
Soft eyes of friendly deer in peaceful grove?

Priyamvada. Sir, we are under bonds to lead a life of virtue. But it is her father's wish to give her to a suitable lover.

King (*joyfully to himself*).

O heart, your wish is won!
All doubt at last is done;
The thing you feared as fire,
Is the jewel of your desire.

Shakuntala (*pettishly*). Anusuya, I'm going.

Anusuya. What for?

Shakuntala. I am going to tell Mother Gautami that Priyamvada is talking nonsense. (*She rises.*)

Anusuya. My dear, we hermit people cannot neglect to entertain a distinguished guest, and go wandering about.

(SHAKUNTALA *starts to walk away without answering.*)

King (*aside*). She is going! (*He starts up as if to detain her, then checks his desires.*) A thought is as vivid as an act, to a lover.

Though nurture, conquering nature, holds
Me back, it seems
As had I started and returned
In waking dreams.

Priyamvada (*approaching* SHAKUNTALA). You dear, peevish girl! You mustn't go.

Shakuntala (*turns with a frown*). Why not?

Priyamvada. You owe me the watering of two trees. You can go when you have paid your debt. (*She forces her to come back.*)

King. It is plain that she is already wearied by watering the trees. See!

Her shoulders droop; her palms are reddened yet;
Quick breaths are struggling in her bosom fair;
The blossom o'er her ear hangs limply wet;
One hand restrains the loose, dishevelled hair.

I therefore remit her debt. (*He gives the two friends a ring. They take it, read the name engraved on it, and look at each other.*)

King. Make no mistake. This is a present—from the king.

Priyamvada. Then, sir, you ought not to part with it. Your word is enough to remit the debt.

Anusuya. Well, Shakuntala, you are set free by this kind gentleman—or rather, by the king himself. Where are you going now?

Shakuntala (*to herself*). I would never leave him if I could help myself.

Priyamvada. Why don't you go now?

Shakuntala. I am not *your* servant any longer. I will go when I like.

King (*looking at* SHAKUNTALA. *To himself*). Does she feel toward me as I do toward her? At least, there is ground for hope.

Although she does not speak to me,
She listens while I speak;
Her eyes turn not to see my face,
But nothing else they seek.

A voice behind the scenes. Hermits! Hermits! Prepare to defend the creatures in our pious grove. King Dushyanta is hunting in the neighbourhood.

The dust his horses' hoofs have raised,
Red as the evening sky,
Falls like a locust-swarm on boughs
Where hanging garments dry.

King (*aside*). Alas! My soldiers are disturbing the pious grove in their search for me.

The voice behind the scenes. Hermits! Hermits! Here is an elephant who is terrifying old men, women, and children.

One tusk is splintered by a cruel blow
Against a blocking tree; his gait is slow,
For countless fettering vines impede and cling;
He puts the deer to flight; some evil thing
He seems, that comes our peaceful life to mar,
Fleeing in terror from the royal car.

(*The girls listen and rise anxiously.*)

King. I have offended sadly against the hermits. I must go back.

The two friends. Your Honour, we are frightened by this alarm of the elephant. Permit us to return to the cottage.

Anusuya (*to* SHAKUNTALA). Shakuntala dear, Mother Gautami will be anxious. We must hurry and find her.

Shakuntala (*feigning lameness*). Oh, oh! I can hardly walk.

King. You must go very slowly. And I will take pains that the hermitage is not disturbed.

The two friends. Your honour, we feel as if we knew you very well. Pray pardon our shortcomings as hostesses. May we ask you to seek better entertainment from us another time?

King. You are too modest. I feel honoured by the mere sight of you.

Shakuntala. Anusuya, my foot is cut on a sharp blade of grass, and my dress is caught on an amaranth twig. Wait for me while I loosen it. (*She casts a lingering glance at the king, and goes out with her two friends.*)

King (*sighing*). They are gone. And I must go. The sight of Shakuntala has made me dread the return to the city. I will make my men camp at a distance from the pious grove. But I cannot turn my own thoughts from Shakuntala.

It is my body leaves my love, not I;
My body moves away, but not my mind;
For back to her my struggling fancies fly
Like silken banners borne against the wind.

(Exit.)

ACT
II
THE SECRET

(*Enter the clown.*)

Clown (*sighing*). Damn! Damn! Damn! I'm tired of being friends with this sporting king. "There's a deer!" he shouts, "There's a boar!" And off he chases on a summer noon through woods where shade is few and far between. We drink hot, stinking water from the mountain streams, flavoured with leaves—nasty! At odd times we get a little tepid meat to eat. And the horses and the elephants make such a noise that I can't even be comfortable at night. Then the hunters and the bird-chasers—damn 'em—wake me up bright and early. They do make an ear-splitting rumpus when they start for the woods. But even that isn't the whole misery. There's a new pimple growing on the old boil. He left us behind and went hunting a deer. And there in a hermitage they say he found—oh, dear! oh, dear! he found a hermit-girl named Shakuntala. Since then he hasn't a thought of going back to town. I lay awake all night, thinking about it. What can I do? Well, I'll see my friend when he is dressed and beautified. (*He walks and looks about.*) Hello! Here he comes, with his bow in his hand, and his girl in his heart. He is wearing a wreath of wild flowers! I'll pretend to be all knocked up. Perhaps I can get a rest that way. (*He stands, leaning on his staff. Enter the king, as described.*)

King (*to himself*).

Although my darling is not lightly won,
She seemed to love me, and my hopes are bright;

Though love be balked ere joy be well begun,
A common longing is itself delight.

(*Smiling.*) Thus does a lover deceive himself. He judges his love's feelings by his own desires.

Her glance was loving—but 'twas not for me;
Her step was slow—'twas grace, not coquetry;
Her speech was short—to her detaining friend.
In things like these love reads a selfish end!

Clown (*standing as before*). Well, king, I can't move my hand. I can only greet you with my voice.

King (*looking and smiling*). What makes you lame?

Clown. Good! You hit a man in the eye, and then ask him why the tears come.

King. I do not understand you. Speak plainly.

Clown. When a reed bends over like a hunchback, do you blame the reed or the river-current?

King. The river-current, of course.

Clown. And you are to blame for my troubles.

King. How so?

Clown. It's a fine thing for you to neglect your royal duties and such a sure job—to live in the woods! What's the good of talking? Here I am, a Brahman, and my joints are all shaken up by this eternal running after wild animals, so that I can't move. Please be good to me. Let us have a rest for just one day.

King (*to himself*). He says this. And I too, when I remember Kanva's daughter, have little desire for the chase. For

The bow is strung, its arrow near;
And yet I cannot bend
That bow against the fawns who share
Soft glances with their friend.

Clown (*observing the king*). He means more than he says. I might as well weep in the woods.

King (*smiling*). What more could I mean? I have been thinking that I ought to take my friend's advice.

Clown (*cheerfully*). Long life to you, then. (*He unstiffens.*)

King. Wait. Hear me out.

Clown. Well, sir?

King. When you are rested, you must be my companion in another task—an easy one.

Clown. Crushing a few sweetmeats?

King. I will tell you presently.

Clown. Pray command my leisure.

King. Who stands without? (*Enter the door-keeper.*)

Door-keeper. I await your Majesty's commands.

King. Raivataka, summon the general.

Door-keeper. Yes, your Majesty. (*He goes out, then returns with the general.*) Follow me, sir. There is his Majesty, listening to our conversation. Draw near, sir.

General (*observing the king, to himself*). Hunting is declared to be a sin, yet it brings nothing but good to the king. See!

He does not heed the cruel sting
Of his recoiling, twanging string;
The mid-day sun, the dripping sweat
Affect him not, nor make him fret;
His form, though sinewy and spare,
Is most symmetrically fair;
No mountain-elephant could be
More filled with vital strength than he.

(*He approaches.*) Victory to your Majesty! The forest is full of deer-tracks, and beasts of prey cannot be far off. What better occupation could we have?

King. Bhadrasena, my enthusiasm is broken. Madhavya has been preaching against hunting.

General (*aside to the clown*). Stick to it, friend Madhavya. I will humour the king a moment. (*Aloud.*) Your Majesty, he is a chattering idiot. Your Majesty may judge by his own case whether hunting is an evil. Consider:

The hunter's form grows sinewy, strong, and light;
He learns, from beasts of prey, how wrath and fright
Affect the mind; his skill he loves to measure
With moving targets. 'Tis life's chiefest pleasure.

Clown (*angrily*). Get out! Get out with your strenuous life! The king has come to his senses. But you, you son of a slave-wench, can go chasing from forest to forest, till you fall into the jaws of some old bear that is looking for a deer or a jackal.

King. Bhadrasena, I cannot take your advice, because I am in the vicinity of a hermitage. So for to-day

The hornèd buffalo may shake
The turbid water of the lake;
Shade-seeking deer may chew the cud,
Boars trample swamp-grass in the mud;
The bow I bend in hunting, may
Enjoy a listless holiday.

General. Yes, your Majesty.

King. Send back the archers who have gone ahead. And forbid the soldiers to vex the hermitage, or even to approach it. Remember:

There lurks a hidden fire in each
Religious hermit-bower;
Cool sun-stones kindle if assailed
By any foreign power.

General. Yes, your Majesty.

Clown. Now will you get out with your strenuous life? (*Exit general.*)

King (*to his attendants*). Lay aside your hunting dress. And you, Raivataka, return to your post of duty.

Raivataka. Yes, your Majesty. (*Exit.*)

Clown. You have got rid of the vermin. Now be seated on this flat stone, over which the trees spread their canopy of shade. I can't sit down till you do.

King. Lead the way.

Clown. Follow me. (*They walk about and sit down.*)

King. Friend Madhavya, you do not know what vision is. You have not seen the fairest of all objects.

Clown. I see you, right in front of me.

King. Yes, every one thinks himself beautiful. But I was speaking of Shakuntala, the ornament of the hermitage.

Clown (*to himself*). I mustn't add fuel to the flame. (*Aloud.*) But you can't have her because she is a hermit-girl. What is the use of seeing her?

King. Fool!

And is it selfish longing then,
That draws our souls on high
Through eyes that have forgot to wink,
As the new moon climbs the sky?

Besides, Dushyanta's thoughts dwell on no forbidden object.

Clown. Well, tell me about her.

King.

Sprung from a nymph of heaven
Wanton and gay,

Who spurned the blessing given,
Going her way;

By the stern hermit taken
In her most need:
So fell the blossom shaken,
Flower on a weed.

Clown. (*laughing*). You are like a man who gets tired of good dates and longs for sour tamarind. All the pearls of the palace are yours, and you want this girl!

King. My friend, you have not seen her, or you could not talk so.

Clown. She must be charming if she surprises *you*.

King. Oh, my friend, she needs not many words.

She is God's vision, of pure thought
Composed in his creative mind;
His reveries of beauty wrought
The peerless pearl of womankind.
So plays my fancy when I see
How great is God, how lovely she.

Clown. How the women must hate her!

King. This too is in my thought.

She seems a flower whose fragrance none has tasted,
A gem uncut by workman's tool,
A branch no desecrating hands have wasted,
Fresh honey, beautifully cool.

No man on earth deserves to taste her beauty,
Her blameless loveliness and worth,

Unless he has fulfilled man's perfect duty—
And is there such a one on earth?

Clown. Marry her quick, then, before the poor girl falls into the hands of some oily-headed hermit.

King. She is dependent on her father, and he is not here.

Clown. But how does she feel toward you?

King. My friend, hermit-girls are by their very nature timid. And yet

When I was near, she could not look at me;
She smiled—but not to me—and half denied it;
She would not show her love for modesty,
Yet did not try so very hard to hide it.

Clown. Did you want her to climb into your lap the first time she saw you?

King. But when she went away with her friends, she almost showed that she loved me.

When she had hardly left my side,
"I cannot walk," the maiden cried,
And turned her face, and feigned to free
The dress not caught upon the tree.

Clown. She has given you some memories to chew on. I suppose that is why you are so in love with the pious grove.

King. My friend, think of some pretext under which we may return to the hermitage.

Clown. What pretext do you need? Aren't you the king?

King. What of that?

Clown. Collect the taxes on the hermits' rice.

King. Fool! It is a very different tax which these hermits pay—one that outweighs heaps of gems.

The wealth we take from common men,
Wastes while we cherish;
These share with us such holiness
As ne'er can perish.

Voices behind the scenes. Ah, we have found him.

King (*Listening*). The voices are grave and tranquil. These must be hermits. (*Enter the door-keeper.*)

Door-keeper. Victory, O King. There are two hermit-youths at the gate.

King. Bid them enter at once.

Door-keeper. Yes, your Majesty. (*He goes out, then returns with the youths.*) Follow me.

First youth (*looking at the king*). A majestic presence, yet it inspires confidence. Nor is this wonderful in a king who is half a saint. For to him

The splendid palace serves as hermitage;
His royal government, courageous, sage,
Adds daily to his merit; it is given
To him to win applause from choirs of heaven
Whose anthems to his glory rise and swell,
Proclaiming him a king, and saint as well.

Second youth. My friend, is this Dushyanta, friend of Indra?

First youth. It is.

Second youth.

Nor is it wonderful that one whose arm
Might bolt a city gate, should keep from harm
The whole broad earth dark-belted by the sea;
For when the gods in heaven with demons fight,
Dushyanta's bow and Indra's weapon bright
Are their reliance for the victory.

The two youths (*approaching*). Victory, O King!

King (*rising*). I salute you.

The two youths. All hail! (*They offer fruit.*)

King (*receiving it and bowing low*). May I know the reason of your coming?

The two youths. The hermits have learned that you are here, and they request—

King. They command rather.

The two youths. The powers of evil disturb our pious life in the absence of the hermit-father. We therefore ask that you will remain a few nights with your charioteer to protect the hermitage.

King. I shall be most happy to do so.

Clown (*to the king*). You rather seem to like being collared this way.

King. Raivataka, tell my charioteer to drive up, and to bring the bow and arrows.

Raivataka. Yes, your Majesty. (*Exit*)

The two youths.

> Thou art a worthy scion of
> The kings who ruled our nation
> And found, defending those in need,
> Their truest consecration.

King. Pray go before. And I will follow straightway.

The two youths. Victory, O King! (*Exeunt.*)

King. Madhavya, have you no curiosity to see Shakuntala?

Clown. I *did* have an unending curiosity, but this talk about the powers of evil has put an end to it.

King. Do not fear. You will be with me.

Clown. I'll stick close to your chariot-wheel. (*Enter the door-keeper.*)

Door-keeper. Your Majesty, the chariot is ready, and awaits your departure to victory. But one Karabhaka has come from the city, a messenger from the queen-mother.

King (*respectfully*). Sent by my mother?

Door-keeper. Yes.

King. Let him enter.

Door-keeper (*goes out and returns with* KARABHAKA). Karabhaka, here is his Majesty. You may draw near.

Karabhaka (*approaching and bowing low*). Victory to your Majesty. The queen-mother sends her commands—

King. What are her commands?

Karabhaka. She plans to end a fasting ceremony on the fourth day from to-day. And on that occasion her dear son must not fail to wait upon her.

King. On the one side is my duty to the hermits, on the other my mother's command. Neither may be disregarded. What is to be done?

Clown (*laughing*). Stay half-way between, like Trishanku.

King. In truth, I am perplexed.

Two inconsistent duties sever
My mind with cruel shock,
As when the current of a river
Is split upon a rock.

(*He reflects.*) My friend, the queen-mother has always felt toward you as toward a son. Do you return, tell her what duty keeps me here, and yourself perform the offices of a son.

Clown. You don't think I am afraid of the devils?

King (*smiling*). O mighty Brahman, who could suspect it?

Clown. But I want to travel like a prince.

King. I will send all the soldiers with you, for the pious grove must not be disturbed. *Clown* (*strutting*). Aha! Look at the heir-apparent!

King (*to himself*). The fellow is a chatterbox. He might betray my longing to the ladies of the palace. Good, then! (*He takes the clown by the hand. Aloud.*) Friend Madhavya, my reverence for the hermits draws me to the hermitage. Do not think that I am really in love with the hermit-girl. Just think:

A king, and a girl of the calm hermit-grove,
Bred with the fawns, and a stranger to love!
Then do not imagine a serious quest;
The light words I uttered were spoken in jest.

Clown. Oh, I understand that well enough. (*Exeunt ambo.*)

ACT
III
THE LOVE-MAKING

(*Enter a pupil, with sacred grass for the sacrifice.*)

Pupil (*with meditative astonishment*). How great is the power of King Dushyanta! Since his arrival our rites have been undisturbed.

He does not need to bend the bow;
For every evil thing,
Awaiting not the arrow, flees
From the twanging of the string.

Well, I will take this sacred grass to the priests, to strew the altar. (*He walks and looks about, then speaks to some one not visible.*) Priyamvada, for whom are you carrying this cuscus-salve and the fibrous lotus-leaves? (*He listens.*) What do you say? That Shakuntala has become seriously ill from the heat, and that these things are to relieve her suffering? Give her the best of care, Priyamvada. She is the very life of the hermit-father. And I will give Gautami the holy water for her. (*Exit. Enter the lovelorn king.*)

King (*with a meditative sigh*).

I know that stern religion's power
Keeps guardian watch my maiden o'er;
Yet all my heart flows straight to her
Like water to the valley-floor.

Oh, mighty Love, thine arrows are made of flowers. How can they be so sharp? (*He recalls something.*) Ah, I understand.

Shiva's devouring wrath still burns in thee,
As burns the eternal fire beneath the sea;
Else how couldst thou, thyself long since consumed,
Kindle the fire that flames so ruthlessly?

Indeed, the moon and thou inspire confidence, only to deceive the host of lovers.

Thy shafts are blossoms; coolness streams
From moon-rays: thus the poets sing;
But to the lovelorn, falsehood seems
To lurk in such imagining;
The moon darts fire from frosty beams;
Thy flowery arrows cut and sting.

And yet

If Love will trouble her
Whose great eyes madden me,
I greet him unafraid,
Though wounded ceaselessly.

O mighty god, wilt thou not show me mercy after such reproaches?

With tenderness unending
I cherished thee when small,
In vain—thy bow is bending;
On me thine arrows fall.
My care for thee to such a plight
Has brought me; and it serves me right.

I have driven off the powers of evil, and the hermits have dismissed me. Where shall I go now to rest from my weariness? (*He sighs.*) There is no rest for me except in seeing her whom I love. (*He looks up.*) She usually spends these hours of midday heat with her friends on the vine-wreathed banks of the Malini. I will go there. (*He walks and looks about.*) I believe the slender maiden has just passed through this corridor of young trees. For

The stems from which she gathered flowers
Are still unhealed;
The sap where twigs were broken off
Is uncongealed.

(*He feels a breeze stirring.*) This is a pleasant spot, with the wind among the trees.

Limbs that love's fever seizes,
Their fervent welcome pay
To lotus-fragrant breezes
That bear the river-spray.

(*He studies the ground.*) Ah, Shakuntala must be in this reedy bower. For

In white sand at the door
Fresh footprints appear,
The toe lightly outlined,
The heel deep and clear.

I will hide among the branches, and see what happens. (*He does so. Joyfully.*) Ah, my eyes have found their heaven. Here is the darling of my thoughts, lying upon a flower-strewn bench of stone, and attended by her two friends. I will hear what they say to each other. (*He stands gazing. Enter* SHAKUNTALA *with her two friends.*)

The two friends (*fanning her*). Do you feel better, dear, when we fan you with these lotus-leaves?

Shakuntala (*wearily*). Oh, are you fanning me, my dear girls? (*The two friends look sorrowfully at each other.*)

King. She is seriously ill. (*Doubtfully.*) Is it the heat, or is it as I hope? (*Decidedly.*) It *must* be so.

With salve upon her breast,
With loosened lotus-chain,
My darling, sore oppressed,
Is lovely in her pain.

Though love and summer heat
May work an equal woe,
No maiden seems so sweet
When summer lays her low.

Priyamvada (*aside to* ANUSUYA). Anusuya, since she first saw the good king, she has been greatly troubled. I do not believe her fever has any other cause.

Anusuya. I suspect you are right. I am going to ask her. My dear, I must ask you something. You are in a high fever.

King. It is too true.

Her lotus-chains that were as white
As moonbeams shining in the night,
Betray the fever's awful pain,
And fading, show a darker stain.

Shakuntala (*half-rising*) Well, say whatever you like.

Anusuya. Shakuntala dear, you have not told us what is going on in your mind. But I have heard old, romantic stories, and I can't help thinking that you are in a state like that of a lady in love.

Please tell us what hurts you. We have to understand the disease before we can even try to cure it.

King. Anusuya expresses my own thoughts.

Shakuntala. It hurts me terribly. I can't tell you all at once.

Priyamvada. Anusuya is right, dear. Why do you hide your trouble? You are wasting away every day. You are nothing but a beautiful shadow.

King. Priyamvada is right. See!

Her cheeks grow thin; her breast and shoulders fail;
Her waist is weary and her face is pale:
She fades for love; oh, pitifully sweet!
As vine-leaves wither in the scorching heat.

Shakuntala (*sighing*). I could not tell any one else. But I shall be a burden to you.

The two friends. That is why we insist on knowing, dear. Grief must be shared to be endured.

King.

To friends who share her joy and grief
She tells what sorrow laid her here;
She turned to look her love again
When first I saw her—yet I fear!

Shakuntala. Ever since I saw the good king who protects the pious grove—(*She stops and fidgets.*)

The two friends. Go on, dear.

Shakuntala. I love him, and it makes me feel like this.

The two friends. Good, good! You have found a lover worthy of your devotion. But of course, a great river always runs into the sea.

King (*joyfully*). I have heard what I longed to hear.

'Twas love that caused the burning pain;
'Tis love that eases it again;
As when, upon a sultry day,
Rain breaks, and washes grief away.

Shakuntala. Then, if you think best, make the good king take pity upon me. If not, remember that I was. *King*. Her words end all doubt.

Priyamvada (*aside to* ANUSUYA). Anusuya, she is far gone in love and cannot endure any delay.

Anusuya. Priyamvada, can you think of any scheme by which we could carry out her wishes quickly and secretly?

Priyamvada. We must plan about the "secretly." The "quickly" is not hard.

Anusuya. How so?

Priyamvada. Why, the good king shows his love for her in his tender glances, and he has been wasting away, as if he were losing sleep.

King. It is quite true.

The hot tears, flowing down my cheek
All night on my supporting arm
And on its golden bracelet, seek
To stain the gems and do them harm.

The bracelet slipping o'er the scars
Upon the wasted arm, that show
My deeds in hunting and in wars,
All night is moving to and fro.

Priyamvada (*reflecting*). Well, she must write him a love-letter. And I will hide it in a bunch of flowers and see that it gets into the king's hand as if it were a relic of the sacrifice.

Anusuya. It is a pretty plan, dear, and it pleases me. What does Shakuntala say?

Shakuntala. I suppose I must obey orders.

Priyamvada. Then compose a pretty little love-song, with a hint of yourself in it.

Shakuntala. I'll try. But my heart trembles, for fear he will despise me.

King.

Here stands the eager lover, and you pale
For fear lest he disdain a love so kind:
The seeker may find fortune, or may fail;
But how could fortune, seeking, fail to find?

And again:

The ardent lover comes, and yet you fear
Lest he disdain love's tribute, were it brought,
The hope of which has led his footsteps here—
Pearls need not seek, for they themselves are sought.

The two friends. You are too modest about your own charms. Would anybody put up a parasol to keep off the soothing autumn moonlight?

Shakuntala (*smiling*). I suppose I shall have to obey orders. (*She meditates*.)

King. It is only natural that I should forget to wink when I see my darling. For

One clinging eyebrow lifted,
As fitting words she seeks,
Her face reveals her passion
For me in glowing cheeks.

Shakuntala. Well, I have thought out a little song. But I haven't anything to write with.

Priyamvada. Here is a lotus-leaf, glossy as a parrot's breast. You can cut the letters in it with your nails.

Shakuntala. Now listen, and tell me whether it makes sense.

The two friends. Please.

Shakuntala (*reads*).

I know not if I read your heart aright;
Why, pitiless, do you distress me so?
I only know that longing day and night
Tosses my restless body to and fro,
That yearns for you, the source of all its woe.

King (*advancing*).

Though Love torments you, slender maid,
Yet he consumes me quite,
As daylight shuts night-blooming flowers
And slays the moon outright.

The two friends (*perceive the king and rise joyfully*). Welcome to the wish that is fulfilled without delay. (SHAKUNTALA *tries to rise.*)

King.

Do not try to rise, beautiful Shakuntala.
Your limbs from which the strength is fled,
That crush the blossoms of your bed
And bruise the lotus-leaves, may be
Pardoned a breach of courtesy.

Shakuntala (*sadly to herself*). Oh, my heart, you were so impatient, and now you find no answer to make.

Anusuya. Your Majesty, pray do this stone bench the honour of sitting upon it. (SHAKUNTALA *edges away*.)

King (*seating himself*). Priyamvada, I trust your friend's illness is not dangerous.

Priyamvada (*smiling*). A remedy is being applied and it will soon be better. It is plain, sir, that you and she love each other. But I love her too, and I must say something over again.

King. Pray do not hesitate. It always causes pain in the end, to leave unsaid what one longs to say.

Priyamvada. Then listen, sir.

King. I am all attention.

Priyamvada. It is the king's duty to save hermit-folk from all suffering. Is not that good Scripture?

King. There is no text more urgent.

Priyamvada. Well, our friend has been brought to this sad state by her love for you. Will you not take pity on her and save her life?

King. We cherish the same desire. I feel it a great honour.

Shakuntala (*with a jealous smile*). Oh, don't detain the good king. He is separated from the court ladies, and he is anxious to go back to them.

King.

Bewitching eyes that found my heart,
You surely see
It could no longer live apart,
Nor faithless be.
I bear Love's arrows as I can;
Wound not with doubt a wounded man.

Anusuya. But, your Majesty, we hear that kings have many favourites. You must act in such a way that our friend may not become a cause of grief to her family.

King. What more can I say?

Though many queens divide my court,
But two support the throne;
Your friend will find a rival in
The sea-girt earth alone.

The two friends. We are content. (SHAKUNTALA *betrays her joy.*) *Priyamvada* (*aside to* ANUSUYA). Look, Anusuya! See how the dear girl's life is coming back moment by moment—just like a peahen in summer when the first rainy breezes come.

Shakuntala. You must please ask the king's pardon for the rude things we said when we were talking together.

The two friends (*smiling*). Anybody who says it was rude, may ask his pardon. Nobody else feels guilty.

Shakuntala. Your Majesty, pray forgive what we said when we did not know that you were present. I am afraid that we say a great many things behind a person's back.

King (*smiling*).

Your fault is pardoned if I may
Relieve my weariness
By sitting on the flower-strewn couch
Your fevered members press.

Priyamvada. But that will not be enough to satisfy him.

Shakuntala (*feigning anger*). Stop! You are a rude girl. You make fun of me when I am in this condition.

Anusuya (*looking out of the arbour*). Priyamvada, there is a little fawn, looking all about him. He has probably lost his mother and is trying to find her. I am going to help him.

Priyamvada. He is a frisky little fellow. You can't catch him alone. I'll go with you. (*They start to go.*)

Shakuntala. I will not let you go and leave me alone.

The two friends (*smiling*). You alone, when the king of the world is with you! (*Exeunt.*)

Shakuntala. Are my friends gone?

King (*looking about*). Do not be anxious, beautiful Shakuntala. Have you not a humble servant here, to take the place of your friends? Then tell me:

Shall I employ the moistened lotus-leaf
To fan away your weariness and grief?
Or take your lily feet upon my knee
And rub them till you rest more easily?

Shakuntala. I will not offend against those to whom I owe honour. (*She rises weakly and starts to walk away.*) *King* (*detaining her*). The day is still hot, beautiful Shakuntala, and you are feverish.

Leave not the blossom-dotted couch
To wander in the midday heat,
With lotus-petals on your breast,
With fevered limbs and stumbling feet.

(*He lays his hand upon her.*)

Shakuntala. Oh, don't! Don't! For I am not mistress of myself. Yet what can I do now? I had no one to help me but my friends.

King. I am rebuked.

Shakuntala. I was not thinking of your Majesty. I was accusing fate.

King. Why accuse a fate that brings what you desire?

1*Shakuntala*. Why not accuse a fate that robs me of self-control and tempts me with the virtues of another?

King (*to himself*).

Though deeply longing, maids are coy
And bid their wooers wait;
Though eager for united joy
In love, they hesitate.

Love cannot torture them, nor move
Their hearts to sudden mating;
Perhaps they even torture love
By their procrastinating.

(SHAKUNTALA *moves away.*)

King. Why should I not have my way? (*He approaches and seizes her dress.*)

Shakuntala. Oh, sir! Be a gentleman. There are hermits wandering about.

King. Do not fear your family, beautiful Shakuntala. Father Kanva knows the holy law. He will not regret it.

For many a hermit maiden who
By simple, voluntary rite
Dispensed with priest and witness, yet
Found favour in her father's sight.

(*He looks about.*) Ah, I have come into the open air. (*He leaves* SHAKUNTALA *and retraces his steps.*) *Shakuntala* (*takes a step, then turns with an eager gesture*).

O King, I cannot do as you would have me. You hardly know me after this short talk. But oh, do not forget me.

King.

When evening comes, the shadow of the tree
Is cast far forward, yet does not depart;
Even so, belovèd, wheresoe'er you be,
The thought of you can never leave my heart.

Shakuntala (*takes a few steps. To herself*). Oh, oh! When I hear him speak so, my feet will not move away. I will hide in this amaranth hedge and see how long his love lasts. (*She hides and waits.*)

King. Oh, my belovèd, my love for you is my whole life, yet you leave me and go away without a thought.

Your body, soft as siris-flowers,
Engages passion's utmost powers;
How comes it that your heart is hard
As stalks that siris-blossoms guard?

Shakuntala. When I hear this, I have no power to go.

King. What have I to do here, where she is not? (*He gazes on the ground.*) Ah, I cannot go.

The perfumed lotus-chain
That once was worn by her
Fetters and keeps my heart
A hopeless prisoner. (*He lifts it reverently.*)

Shakuntala (*looking at her arm*). Why, I was so weak and ill that when the lotus-bracelet fell off, I did not even notice it.

King (*laying the lotus-bracelet on his heart*). Ah!

Once, dear, on your sweet arm it lay,
And on my heart shall ever stay;
Though you disdain to give me joy,
I find it in a lifeless toy.

Shakuntala. I cannot hold back after that. I will use the bracelet as an excuse for my coming. (*She approaches.*)

King (*seeing her. Joyfully*). The queen of my life! As soon as I complained, fate proved kind to me.

No sooner did the thirsty bird
With parching throat complain,
Than forming clouds in heaven stirred
And sent the streaming rain.

Shakuntala (*standing before the king*). When I was going away, sir, I remembered that this lotus-bracelet had fallen from my arm, and I have come back for it. My heart seemed to tell me that you had taken it. Please give it back, or you will betray me, and yourself too, to the hermits.

King. I will restore it on one condition.

Shakuntala. What condition?

King. That I may myself place it where it belongs.

Shakuntala (*to herself*). What can I do? (*She approaches.*)

King. Let us sit on this stone bench. (*They walk to the bench and sit down.*)

King (*taking* SHAKUNTALA'S *hand*). Ah!

When Shiva's anger burned the tree
Of love in quenchless fire,
Did heavenly fate preserve a shoot
To deck my heart's desire?

Shakuntala (*feeling his touch*). Hasten, my dear, hasten.

King (*joyfully to himself*). Now I am content. She speaks as a wife to her husband. (*Aloud.*) Beautiful Shakuntala, the clasp of the bracelet is not very firm. May I fasten it in another way?

Shakuntala (*smiling*). If you like.

King (*artfully delaying before he fastens it*). See, my beautiful girl!

The lotus-chain is dazzling white
As is the slender moon at night.
Perhaps it was the moon on high
That joined her horns and left the sky,
Believing that your lovely arm
Would, more than heaven, enhance her charm.

Shakuntala. I cannot see it. The pollen from the lotus over my ear has blown into my eye.

King (*smiling*). Will you permit me to blow it away?

Shakuntala. I should not like to be an object of pity. But why should I not trust you? *King*. Do not have such thoughts. A new servant does not transgress orders.

Shakuntala. It is this exaggerated courtesy that frightens me.

King (*to himself*). I shall not break the bonds of this sweet servitude. (*He starts to raise her face to his.* SHAKUNTALA *resists a little, then is passive.*)

King. Oh, my bewitching girl, have no fear of me.

(SHAKUNTALA *darts a glance at him, then looks down. The king raises her face. Aside.*)

Her sweetly trembling lip
With virgin invitation
Provokes my soul to sip
Delighted fascination.

Shakuntala. You seem slow, dear, in fulfilling your promise.

King. The lotus over your ear is so near your eye, and so like it, that I was confused. (*He gently blows her eye.*)

Shakuntala. Thank you. I can see quite well now. But I am ashamed not to make any return for your kindness.

King. What more could I ask?

It ought to be enough for me
To hover round your fragrant face;
Is not the lotus-haunting bee
Content with perfume and with grace?

Shakuntala. But what does he do if he is not content?

King. This! This! (*He draws her face to his.*)

A voice behind the scenes. O sheldrake bride, bid your mate farewell. The night is come.

Shakuntala (listening excitedly). Oh, my dear, this is Mother Gautami, come to inquire about me. Please hide among the branches. (*The king conceals himself. Enter* GAUTAMI, *with a bowl in her hand.*)

Gautami. Here is the holy water, my child. (*She sees* SHAKUNTALA *and helps her to rise.*) So ill, and all alone here with the gods?

Shakuntala. It was just a moment ago that Priyamvada and Anusuya went down to the river.

Gautami (sprinkling SHAKUNTALA *with the holy water)*. May you live long and happy, my child. Has the fever gone down? (*She touches her.*)

Shakuntala. There is a difference, mother.

Gautami. The sun is setting. Come, let us go to the cottage.

Shakuntala (weakly rising. To herself). Oh, my heart, you delayed when your desire came of itself. Now see what you have done. (*She takes a step, then turns around. Aloud.*) O bower that took away my pain, I bid you farewell until another blissful hour. (*Exeunt* SHAKUNTALA *and* GAUTAMI.)

King (advancing with a sigh.) The path to happiness is strewn with obstacles.

Her face, adorned with soft eye-lashes,
Adorable with trembling flashes
Of half-denial, in memory lingers;
The sweet lips guarded by her fingers,
The head that drooped upon her shoulder—
Why was I not a little bolder?

Where shall I go now? Let me stay a moment in this bower where my belovèd lay. (*He looks about.*)

The flower-strewn bed whereon her body tossed;
The bracelet, fallen from her arm and lost;

The dear love-missive, in the lotus-leaf
Cut by her nails: assuage my absent grief
And occupy my eyes—I have no power,
Though she is gone, to leave the reedy bower.

(*He reflects.*) Alas! I did wrong to delay when I had found my love. So now

If she will grant me but one other meeting,
I'll not delay; for happiness is fleeting;
So plans my foolish, self-defeated heart;
But when she comes, I play the coward's part.

A voice behind the scenes. O King!

The flames rise heavenward from the evening altar;
And round the sacrifices, blazing high,
Flesh-eating demons stalk, like red cloud-masses,
And cast colossal shadows on the sky.

King (*listens. Resolutely*). Have no fear, hermits. I am here. (*Exit.*)

ACT IV SHAKUNTALA'S DEPARTURE

SCENE I

(*Enter the two friends, gathering flowers.*)

Anusuya. Priyamvada, dear Shakuntala has been properly married by the voluntary ceremony and she has a husband worthy of her. And yet I am not quite satisfied.

Priyamvada. Why not?

Anusuya. The sacrifice is over and the good king was dismissed to-day by the hermits. He has gone back to the city and there he is surrounded by hundreds of court ladies. I wonder whether he will remember poor Shakuntala or not.

Priyamvada. You need not be anxious about that. Such handsome men are sure to be good. But there is something else to think about. I don't know what Father will have to say when he comes back from his pilgrimage and hears about it.

Anusuya. I believe that he will be pleased.

Priyamvada. Why?

Anusuya. Why not? You know he wanted to give his daughter to a lover worthy of her. If fate brings this about of itself, why shouldn't Father be happy?

Priyamvada. I suppose you are right. (*She looks at her flower-basket.*) My dear, we have gathered flowers enough for the sacrifice.

Anusuya. But we must make an offering to the gods that watch over Shakuntala's marriage. We had better gather more.

Priyamvada. Very well. (*They do so.*)

A voice behind the scenes. Who will bid me welcome?

Anusuya (*listening*). My dear, it sounds like a gùest announcing himself.

Priyamvada. Well, Shakuntala is near the cottage. (*Reflecting.*) Ah, but to-day her heart is far away. Come, we must do with the flowers we have. (*They start to walk away.*)

The voice.

Do you dare despise a guest like me?
Because your heart, by loving fancies blinded,
Has scorned a guest in pious life grown old,
Your lover shall forget you though reminded,
Or think of you as of a story told.

(*The two girls listen and show dejection.*)

Priyamvada. Oh, dear! The very thing has happened. The dear, absent-minded girl has offended some worthy man.

Anusuya (*looking ahead*). My dear, this is no ordinary somebody. It is the great sage Durvasas, the irascible. See how he strides away!

Priyamvada. Nothing burns like fire. Run, fall at his feet, bring him back, while I am getting water to wash his feet.

Anusuya. I will. (*Exit.*)

Priyamvada (*stumbling*). There! I stumbled in my excitement, and the flower-basket fell out of my hand. (*She collects the scattered flowers.* ANUSUYA *returns.*)

Anusuya. My dear, he is anger incarnate. Who could appease him? But I softened him a little.

Priyamvada. Even that is a good deal for him. Tell me about it.

Anusuya. When he would not turn back, I fell at his feet and prayed to him. "Holy sir," I said, "remember her former devotion and pardon this offence. Your daughter did not recognise your great and holy power to-day."

Priyamvada. And then—

Anusuya. Then he said: "My words must be fulfilled. But the curse shall be lifted when her lover sees a gem which he has given her for a token." And so he vanished.

Priyamvada. We can breathe again. When the good king went away, he put a ring, engraved with his own name, on Shakuntala's finger to remember him by. That will save her.

Anusuya. Come, we must finish the sacrifice for her. (*They walk about.*)

Priyamvada (*gazing*). Just look, Anusuya! There is the dear girl, with her cheek resting on her left hand. She looks like a painted picture. She is thinking about him. How could she notice a guest when she has forgotten herself?

Anusuya. Priyamvada, we two must keep this thing to ourselves. We must be careful of the dear girl. You know how delicate she is.

Priyamvada. Would any one sprinkle a jasmine-vine with scalding water? (*Exeunt ambo.*)

SCENE II.—*Early Morning*

(*Enter a pupil of* KANVA, *just risen from sleep.*)

Pupil. Father Kanva has returned from his pilgrimage, and has bidden me find out what time it is. I will go into the open air and see how much of the night remains. (*He walks and looks about.*) See! The dawn is breaking. For already

The moon behind the western mount is sinking;
The eastern sun is heralded by dawn;
From heaven's twin lights, their fall and glory linking,
Brave lessons of submission may be drawn.

And again:

Night-blooming lilies, when the moon is hidden,
Have naught but memories of beauty left.
Hard, hard to bear! Her lot whom heaven has bidden
To live alone, of love and lover reft.

And again:

On jujube-trees the blushing dewdrops falter;
The peacock wakes and leaves the cottage thatch;
A deer is rising near the hoof-marked altar,
And stretching, stands, the day's new life to catch.

And yet again:

The moon that topped the loftiest mountain ranges,
That slew the darkness in the midmost sky,
Is fallen from heaven, and all her glory changes:
So high to rise, so low at last to lie!

Anusuya (*entering hurriedly. To herself*). That is just what happens to the innocent. Shakuntala has been treated shamefully by the king. *Pupil.* I will tell Father Kanva that the hour of morning sacrifice is come. (*Exit.*)

Anusuya. The dawn is breaking. I am awake bright and early. But what shall I do now that I am awake? My hands refuse to attend to the ordinary morning tasks. Well, let love take its course. For the dear, pure-minded girl trusted him—the traitor! Perhaps it is not the good king's fault. It must be the curse of Durvasas. Otherwise, how could the good king say such beautiful things, and then let all this time pass without even sending a message? (*She reflects.*) Yes, we must send him the ring he left as a token. But whom shall we ask to take it? The hermits are unsympathetic because they have never suffered. It seemed as if her friends were to blame and so, try as we might, we could not tell Father Kanva that Shakuntala was married to Dushyanta and was expecting a baby. Oh, what shall we do? (*Enter* PRIYAMVADA.)

Priyamvada. Hurry, Anusuya, hurry! We are getting Shakuntala ready for her journey.

Anusuya (*astonished*). What do you mean, my dear?

Priyamuada. Listen. I just went to Shakuntala, to ask if she had slept well.

Anusuya. And then—

Priyamvada. I found her hiding her face for shame, and Father Kanva was embracing her and encouraging her. "My child," he said, "I bring you joy. The offering fell straight in the sacred fire, and auspicious smoke rose toward the sacrificer. My pains for you have proved like instruction given to a good student; they have brought me no regret. This very day I shall give you an escort of hermits and send you to your husband."

Anusuya. But, my dear, who told Father Kanva about it?

Priyamvada. A voice from heaven that recited a verse when he had entered the fire-sanctuary.

Anusuya (*astonished*). What did it say?

Priyamvada. Listen. (*Speaking in good Sanskrit.*)

Know, Brahman, that your child,
Like the fire-pregnant tree,
Bears kingly seed that shall be born
For earth's prosperity.

Anusuya (*hugging* PRIYAMVADA). I am so glad, dear. But my joy is half sorrow when I think that Shakuntala is going to be taken away this very day.

Priyamvada. We must hide our sorrow as best we can. The poor girl must be made happy to-day.

Anusuya. Well, here is a cocoa-nut casket, hanging on a branch of the mango-tree. I put flower-pollen in it for this very purpose. It keeps fresh, you know. Now you wrap it in a lotus-leaf, and I will get yellow pigment and earth from a sacred spot and blades of panic grass for the happy ceremony. (PRIYAMVADA *does so. Exit* ANUSUYA.)

A voice behind the scenes. Gautami, bid the worthy Sharngarava and Sharadvata make ready to escort my daughter Shakuntala.

Priyamvada (*listening*). Hurry, Anusuya, hurry! They are calling the hermits who are going to Hastinapura. (*Enter* ANUSUYA, *with materials for the ceremony.*)

Anusuya. Come, dear, let us go. (*They walk about.*)

Priyamvada (*looking ahead*). There is Shakuntala. She took the ceremonial bath at sunrise, and now the hermit-women are giving her rice-cakes and wishing her happiness. Let's go to her. (*They do so. Enter* SHAKUNTALA *with attendants as described, and* GAUTAMI.)

Shakuntala. Holy women, I salute you.

Gautami. My child, may you receive the happy title "queen," showing that your husband honours you.

Hermit-women. My dear, may you become the mother of a hero. (*Exeunt all but* GAUTAMI.)

The two friends (*approaching*). Did you have a good bath, dear?

Shakuntala. Good morning, girls. Sit here.

The two friends (*seating themselves*). Now stand straight, while we go through the happy ceremony.

Shakuntala. It has happened often enough, but I ought to be very grateful to-day. Shall I ever be adorned by my friends again? (*She weeps.*)

The two friends. You ought not to weep, dear, at this happy time. (*They wipe the tears away and adorn her.*)

Priyamvada. You are so beautiful, you ought to have the finest gems. It seems like an insult to give you these hermitage things.

(*Enter* HARITA, *a hermit-youth with ornaments.*) *Harita.* Here are ornaments for our lady. (*The women look at them in astonishment.*)

Gautami. Harita, my son, whence come these things?

Harita. From the holy power of Father Kanva.

Gautami. A creation of his mind?

Harita. Not quite. Listen. Father Kanva sent us to gather blossoms from the trees for Shakuntala, and then

One tree bore fruit, a silken marriage dress
That shamed the moon in its white loveliness;
Another gave us lac-dye for the feet;
From others, fairy hands extended, sweet
Like flowering twigs, as far as to the wrist,
And gave us gems, to adorn her as we list.

Priyamvada (*Looking at* SHAKUNTALA). A bee may be born in a hole in a tree, but she likes the honey of the lotus.

Gautami. This gracious favour is a token of the queenly happiness which you are to enjoy in your husband's palace. (SHAKUNTALA *shows embarrassment.*)

Harita. Father Kanva has gone to the bank of the Malini, to perform his ablutions. I will tell him of the favour shown us by the trees. (*Exit.*)

Anusuya. My dear, we poor girls never saw such ornaments. How shall we adorn you? (*She stops to think, and to look at the ornaments.*) But we have seen pictures. Perhaps we can arrange them right.

Shakuntala. I know how clever you are. (*The two friends adorn her. Enter* KANVA, *returning after his ablutions.*)

Kanva.

Shakuntala must go to-day;
I miss her now at heart;

I dare not speak a loving word
Or choking tears will start.

My eyes are dim with anxious thought;
Love strikes me to the life:
And yet I strove for pious peace—
I have no child, no wife.

What must a father feel, when come
The pangs of parting from his child at home?

(*He walks about.*) *The two friends*. There, Shakuntala, we have arranged your ornaments. Now put on this beautiful silk dress. (SHAKUNTALA *rises and does so.*)

Gautami. My child, here is your father. The eyes with which he seems to embrace you are overflowing with tears of joy. You must greet him properly. (SHAKUNTALA *makes a shamefaced reverence.*)

Kanva. My child,

Like Sharmishtha, Yayati's wife,
Win favour measured by your worth;
And may you bear a kingly son
Like Puru, who shall rule the earth.

Gautami. My child, this is not a prayer, but a benediction.

Kanva. My daughter, walk from left to right about the fires in which the offering has just been thrown. (*All walk about.*)

The holy fires around the altar kindle,
And at their margins sacred grass is piled;
Beneath their sacrificial odours dwindle
Misfortunes. May the fires protect you, child!

(SHAKUNTALA *walks about them from left to right.*)

Kanva. Now you may start, my daughter. (*He glances about.*) Where are Sharngarava and Sharadvata? (*Enter the two pupils.*)

The two pupils. We are here, Father.

Kanva. Sharngarava, my son, lead the way for your sister.

Sharngarava. Follow me. (*They all walk about.*)

Kanva. O trees of the pious grove, in which the fairies dwell,

She would not drink till she had wet
Your roots, a sister's duty,
Nor pluck your flowers; she loves you yet
Far more than selfish beauty.

'Twas festival in her pure life
When budding blossoms showed;
And now she leaves you as a wife—
Oh, speed her on her road!

Sharngarava (*listening to the song of koïl-birds*). Father,

The trees are answering your prayer
In cooing cuckoo-song,
Bidding Shakuntala farewell,Their sister for so long.

Invisible beings,

May lily-dotted lakes delight your eye;
May shade-trees bid the heat of noonday cease;
May soft winds blow the lotus-pollen nigh;
May all your path be pleasantness and peace.

(*All listen in astonishment.*)

Gautami. My child, the fairies of the pious grove bid you farewell. For they love the household. Pay reverence to the holy ones.

Shakuntala (*does so. Aside to* PRIYAMVADA). Priyamvada, I long to see my husband, and yet my feet will hardly move. It is hard, hard to leave the hermitage.

Priyamvada. You are not the only one to feel sad at this farewell. See how the whole grove feels at parting from you.

The grass drops from the feeding doe;
The peahen stops her dance;
Pale, trembling leaves are falling slow,
The tears of clinging plants.

Shakuntala (*recalling something*). Father, I must say good-bye to the spring-creeper, my sister among the vines.

Kanva. I know your love for her. See! Here she is at your right hand.

Shakuntala (*approaches the vine and embraces it*). Vine sister, embrace me too with your arms, these branches. I shall be far away from you after to-day. Father, you must care for her as you did for me.

Kanva.

My child, you found the lover who
Had long been sought by me;
No longer need I watch for you;
I'll give the vine a lover true,
This handsome mango-tree.

And now start on your journey.

Shakuntala (*going to the two friends*). Dear girls, I leave her in your care too.

The two friends. But who will care for poor us? (*They shed tears.*)

Kanva. Anusuya! Priyamvada! Do not weep. It is you who should cheer Shakuntala. (*All walk about.*)

Shakuntala. Father, there is the pregnant doe, wandering about near the cottage. When she becomes a happy mother, you must send some one to bring me the good news. Do not forget.

Kanva. I shall not forget, my child.

Shakuntala (stumbling) Oh, oh! Who is it that keeps pulling at my dress, as if to hinder me? (*She turns round to see.*)

Kanva.

It is the fawn whose lip, when torn
By kusha-grass, you soothed with oil;
The fawn who gladly nibbled corn
Held in your hand; with loving toil
You have adopted him, and he
Would never leave you willingly.

Shakuntala. My dear, why should you follow me when I am going away from home? Your mother died when you were born and I brought you up. Now I am leaving you, and Father Kanva will take care of you. Go back, dear! Go back! (*She walks away, weeping.*)

Kanva. Do not weep, my child. Be brave. Look at the path before you.

Be brave, and check the rising tears
That dim your lovely eyes;
Your feet are stumbling on the path
That so uneven lies.

Sharngarava. Holy Father, the Scripture declares that one should accompany a departing loved one only to the first water. Pray give us your commands on the bank of this pond, and then return.

Kanva. Then let us rest in the shade of this fig-tree. (*All do so.*) What commands would it be fitting for me to lay on King Dushyanta? (*He reflects.*)

Anusuya. My dear, there is not a living thing in the whole hermitage that is not grieving to-day at saying good-bye to you. Look!

The sheldrake does not heed his mate
Who calls behind the lotus-leaf;
He drops the lily from his bill
And turns on you a glance of grief.

Kanva. Son Sharngarava, when you present Shakuntala to the king, give him this message from me.

Remembering my religious worth,
Your own high race, the love poured forth
By her, forgetful of her friends,
Pay her what honour custom lends
To all your wives. And what fate gives
Beyond, will please her relatives.

Sharngarava. I will not forget your message, Father.

Kanva (*turning to* SHAKUNTALA). My child, I must now give you my counsel. Though I live in the forest, I have some knowledge of the world.

Sharngarava. True wisdom, Father, gives insight into everything.

Kanva. My child, when you have entered your husband's home,

Obey your elders; and be very kind
To rivals; never be perversely blind
And angry with your husband, even though he
Should prove less faithful than a man might be;
Be as courteous to servants as you may,
Not puffed with pride in this your happy day:
Thus does a maiden grow into a wife;
But self-willed women are the curse of life.

But what does Gautami say?

Gautami. This is advice sufficient for a bride. (*To* SHAKUNTALA.) You will not forget, my child.

Kanva. Come, my daughter, embrace me and your friends.

Shakuntala. Oh, Father! Must my friends turn back too?

Kanva. My daughter, they too must some day be given in marriage. Therefore they may not go to court. Gautami will go with you.

Shakuntala (*throwing her arms about her father*). I am torn from my father's breast like a vine stripped from a sandal-tree on the Malabar hills. How can I live in another soil? (*She weeps.*)

Kanva. My daughter, why distress yourself so?

A noble husband's honourable wife,
You are to spend a busy, useful life
In the world's eye; and soon, as eastern skies
Bring forth the sun, from you there shall arise
A child, a blessing and a comfort strong—
You will not miss me, dearest daughter, long.

Shakuntala (*falling at his feet*). Farewell, Father.

Kanva. My daughter, may all that come to you which I desire for you.

Shakuntala (*going to her two friends*). Come, girls! Embrace me, both of you together.

The two friends (*do so*). Dear, if the good king should perhaps be slow to recognise you, show him the ring with his own name engraved on it.

Shakuntala. Your doubts make my heart beat faster.

The two friends. Do not be afraid, dear. Love is timid.

Sharngarava (*looking about*). Father, the sun is in mid-heaven. She must hasten.

Shakuntala (*embracing* KANVA *once more*). Father, when shall I see the pious grove again?

Kanva. My daughter,

When you have shared for many years
The king's thoughts with the earth,
When to a son who knows no fears
You shall have given birth,

When, trusted to the son you love,
Your royal labours cease,
Come with your husband to the grove
And end your days in peace.

Gautami. My child, the hour of your departure is slipping by. Bid your father turn back. No, she would never do that. Pray turn back, sir.

Kanva. Child, you interrupt my duties in the pious grove.

Shakuntala. Yes, Father. You will be busy in the grove. You will not miss me. But oh! I miss you. *Kanva*. How can you think me so indifferent? (*He sighs*.)

My lonely sorrow will not go,
For seeds you scattered here
Before the cottage door, will grow;
And I shall see them, dear.

Go. And peace go with you. (*Exit* SHAKUNTALA, *with* GAUTAMI, SHARNGARAVA, *and* SHARADVATA.)

The two friends (*gazing long after her. Mournfully*). Oh, oh! Shakuntala is lost among the trees.

Kanva. Anusuya! Priyamvada! Your companion is gone. Choke down your grief and follow me. (*They start to go back*.)

The two friends. Father, the grove seems empty without Shakuntala.

Kanva. So love interprets. (*He walks about, sunk in thought.*) Ah! I have sent Shakuntala away, and now I am myself again. For

A girl is held in trust, another's treasure;
To arms of love my child to-day is given;
And now I feel a calm and sacred pleasure;
I have restored the pledge that came from heaven.

(*Exeunt omnes.*)

ACT
V
SHAKUNTALA'S REJECTION

(*Enter a chamberlain.*)

Chamberlain (*sighing*). Alas! To what a state am I reduced!

I once assumed the staff of reed
For custom's sake alone,
As officer to guard at need
The ladies round the throne.
But years have passed away and made
It serve, my tottering steps to aid.

The king is within. I will tell him of the urgent business which demands his attention. (*He takes a few steps.*) But what is the business? (*He recalls it.*) Yes, I remember. Certaiṇ hermits, pupils of Kanva, desire to see his Majesty. Strange, strange!

The mind of age is like a lamp
Whose oil is running thin;
One moment it is shining bright,
Then darkness closes in.

(*He walks and looks about.*) Here is his Majesty.

He does not seek—until a father's care
Is shown his subjects—rest in solitude;

As a great elephant recks not of the sun
Until his herd is sheltered in the wood.

In truth, I hesitate to announce the coming of Kanva's pupils to the king. For he has this moment risen from the throne of justice. But kings are never weary. For

The sun unyokes his horses never;
Blows night and day the breeze;
Shesha upholds the world forever:
And kings are like to these.

(*He walks about. Enter the king, the clown, and retinue according to rank.*) *King* (*betraying the cares of office*). Every one is happy on attaining his desire—except a king. His difficulties increase with his power. Thus:

Security slays nothing but ambition;
With great possessions, troubles gather thick;
Pain grows, not lessens, with a king's position,
As when one's hand must hold the sunshade's stick.

Two court poets behind the scenes. Victory to your Majesty.

First poet.

The world you daily guard and bless,
Not heeding pain or weariness;
Thus is your nature made.
A tree will brave the noonday, when
The sun is fierce, that weary men
May rest beneath its shade.

Second poet.

Vice bows before the royal rod;
Strife ceases at your kingly nod;
You are our strong defender.
Friends come to all whose wealth is sure,
But you, alike to rich and poor,
Are friend both strong and tender.

King (*listening*). Strange! I was wearied by the demands of my office, but this renews my spirit.

Clown. Does a bull forget that he is tired when you call him the leader of the herd?

King (*smiling*). Well, let us sit down. (*They seat themselves, and the retinue arranges itself. A lute is heard behind the scenes.*)

Clown (*listening*). My friend, listen to what is going on in the music-room. Some one is playing a lute, and keeping good time. I suppose Lady Hansavati is practising.

King. Be quiet. I wish to listen.

Chamberlain (*looks at the king*). Ah, the king is occupied. I must await his leisure. (*He stands aside.*)

A song behind the scenes.

You who kissed the mango-flower,
Honey-loving bee,
Gave her all your passion's power,
Ah, so tenderly!

How can you be tempted so
By the lily, pet?
Fresher honey's sweet, I know;
But can you forget?

King. What an entrancing song!

Clown. But, man, don't you understand what the words mean?

King (*smiling*). I was once devoted to Queen Hansavati. And the rebuke comes from her. Friend Madhavya, tell Queen Hansavati in my name that the rebuke is a very pretty one.

Clown. Yes, sir. (*He rises*.) But, man, you are using another fellow's fingers to grab a bear's tail-feathers with. I have about as much chance of salvation as a monk who hasn't forgotten his passions.

King. Go. Soothe her like a gentleman.

Clown. I suppose I must. (*Exit*.)

King (*to himself*). Why am I filled with wistfulness on hearing such a song? I am not separated from one I love. And yet

In face of sweet presentment
Or harmonies of sound,
Man e'er forgets contentment,
By wistful longings bound.

There must be recollections
Of things not seen on earth,
Deep nature's predilections,
Loves earlier than birth.

(*He shows the wistfulness that comes from unremembered things*.)

Chamberlain (*approaching*). Victory to your Majesty. Here are hermits who dwell in the forest at the foot of the Himalayas. They bring women with them, and they carry a message from Kanva. What is your pleasure with regard to them?

King (*astonished*). Hermits? Accompanied by women? From Kanva?

Chamberlain. Yes.

King. Request my chaplain Somarata in my name to receive these hermits in the manner prescribed by Scripture, and to conduct them himself before me. I will await them in a place fit for their reception.

Chamberlain. Yes, your Majesty. (*Exit*.)

King (*rising*). Vetravati, conduct me to the fire-sanctuary.

Portress. Follow me, your Majesty. (*She walks about*) Your Majesty, here is the terrace of the fire-sanctuary. It is beautiful, for it has just been swept, and near at hand is the cow that yields the milk of sacrifice. Pray ascend it.

King (*ascends and stands leaning on the shoulder of an attendant*.) Vetravati, with what purpose does Father Kanva send these hermits to me?

Do leaguèd powers of sin conspire
To balk religion's pure desire?
Has wrong been done to beasts that roam
Contented round the hermits' home?
Do plants no longer bud and flower,
To warn me of abuse of power?
These doubts and more assail my mind,
But leave me puzzled, lost, and blind.

Portress. How could these things be in a hermitage that rests in the fame of the king's arm? No, I imagine they have come to pay homage to their king, and to congratulate him on his pious rule.

(*Enter the chaplain and the chamberlain, conducting the two pupils of* KANVA, *with* GAUTAMI *and* SHAKUNTALA.)

Chamberlain. Follow me, if you please.

Sharngarava. Friend Sharadvata,

The king is noble and to virtue true;
None dwelling here commit the deed of shame;
Yet we ascetics view the worldly crew
As in a house all lapped about with flame.

Sharadvata. Sharngarava, your emotion on entering the city is quite just. As for me,

Free from the world and all its ways,
I see them spending worldly days
As clean men view men smeared with oil,
As pure men, those whom passions soil,
As waking men view men asleep,
As free men, those in bondage deep.

Chaplain. That is why men like you are great.

Shakuntala (*observing an evil omen*). Oh, why does my right eye throb?

Gautami. Heaven avert the omen, my child. May happiness wait upon you. (*They walk about.*)

Chaplain (*indicating the king*). O hermits, here is he who protects those of every station and of every age. He has already risen, and awaits you. Behold him.

Sharngarava. Yes, it is admirable, but not surprising. For

Fruit-laden trees bend down to earth;
The water-pregnant clouds hang low;
Good men are not puffed up by power—
The unselfish are by nature so.

Portress. Your Majesty, the hermits seem to be happy. They give you gracious looks.

King (*observing* SHAKUNTALA). Ah!

Who is she, shrouded in the veil
That dims her beauty's lustre,
Among the hermits like a flower
Round which the dead leaves cluster?

Portress. Your Majesty, she is well worth looking at.

King. Enough! I must not gaze upon another's wife.

Shakuntala (*laying her hand on her breast. Aside*). Oh, my heart, why tremble so? Remember his constant love and be brave.

Chaplain (*advancing*). Hail, your Majesty. The hermits have been received as Scripture enjoins. They have a message from their teacher. May you be pleased to hear it.

King (*respectfully*). I am all attention.

The two pupils (*raising their right hands*). Victory, O King.

King (*bowing low*). I salute you all.

The two pupils. All hail.

King. Does your pious life proceed without disturbance?

The two pupils.

How could the pious duties fail
While you defend the right?
Or how could darkness' power prevail
O'er sunbeams shining bright?

King (*to himself*). Indeed, my royal title is no empty one. (*Aloud.*) Is holy Kanva in health?

Sharngarava. O King, those who have religious power can command health. He asks after your welfare and sends this message.

King. What are his commands?

Sharngarava. He says: "Since you have met this my daughter and have married her, I give you my glad consent. For

You are the best of worthy men, they say;
And she, I know, Good Works personified;
The Creator wrought forever and a day,
In wedding such a virtuous groom and bride.

She is with child. Take her and live with her in virtue."

Gautami. Bless you, sir. I should like to say that no one invites me to speak.

King. Speak, mother.

Gautami.

Did she with father speak or mother?
Did you engage her friends in speech?
Your faith was plighted each to other;
Let each be faithful now to each.

Shakuntala. What will my husband say?

King (*listening with anxious suspicion*). What is this insinuation?

Shakuntala (*to herself*). Oh, oh! So haughty and so slanderous!

Sharngarava. "What is this insinuation?" What is your question? Surely you know the world's ways well enough.

Because the world suspects a wife
Who does not share her husband's lot,
Her kinsmen wish her to abide
With him, although he love her not.

King. You cannot mean that this young woman is my wife.

Shakuntala (*sadly to herself*). Oh, my heart, you feared it, and now it has come. *Sharngarava*. O King,

A king, and shrink when love is done,
Turn coward's back on truth, and flee!

King. What means this dreadful accusation?

Sharngarava (*furiously*).

O drunk with power! We might have knownThat you were steeped in treachery.

King. A stinging rebuke!

Gautami (*to* SHAKUNTALA). Forget your shame, my child. I will remove your veil. Then your husband will recognise you. (*She does so.*)

King (*observing* SHAKUNTALA. *To himself*).

As my heart ponders whether I could ever
Have wed this woman that has come to me
In tortured loveliness, as I endeavour
To bring it back to mind, then like a bee

That hovers round a jasmine flower at dawn,
While frosty dews of morning still o'erweave it,
And hesitates to sip ere they be gone,
I cannot taste the sweet, and cannot leave it.

Portress (*to herself*). What a virtuous king he is! Would any other man hesitate when he saw such a pearl of a woman coming of her own accord?

Sharngarava. Have you nothing to say, O King?

King. Hermit, I have taken thought. I cannot believe that this woman is my wife. She is plainly with child. How can I take her, confessing myself an adulterer?

Shakuntala (*to herself*). Oh, oh, oh! He even casts doubt on our marriage. The vine of my hope climbed high, but it is broken now.

Sharngarava. Not so.

You scorn the sage who rendered whole
His child befouled, and choked his grief,
Who freely gave you what you stole
And added honour to a thief!

Sharadvata. Enough, Sharngarava. Shakuntala, we have said what we were sent to say. You hear his words. Answer him.

Shakuntala (*to herself*). He loved me so. He is so changed. Why remind him? Ah, but I must clear my own character. Well, I will try. (*Aloud*.) My dear husband—(*She stops*.) No, he doubts my right to call him that. Your Majesty, it was pure love that opened my poor heart to you in the hermitage. Then you were kind to me and gave me your promise. Is it right for you to speak so now, and to reject me?

King (*stopping his ears*). Peace, peace!

A stream that eats away the bank,
Grows foul, and undermines the tree.
So you would stain your honour, while
You plunge me into misery.

Shakuntala. Very well. If you have acted so because you really fear to touch another man's wife, I will remove your doubts with a token you gave me.

King. An excellent idea!

Shakuntala (*touching her finger*). Oh, oh! The ring is lost. (*She looks sadly at* GAUTAMI.)

Gautami. My child, you worshipped the holy Ganges at the spot where Indra descended. The ring must have fallen there.

King. Ready wit, ready wit!

Shakuntala. Fate is too strong for me there. I will tell you something else.

King. Let me hear what you have to say.

Shakuntala. One day, in the bower of reeds, you were holding a lotus-leaf cup full of water.

King. I hear you.

Shakuntala. At that moment the fawn came up, my adopted son. Then you took pity on him and coaxed him. "Let him drink first," you said. But he did not know you, and he would not come to drink water from your hand. But he liked it afterwards, when I held the very same water. Then you smiled and said: "It is true. Every one trusts his own sort. You both belong to the forest."

King. It is just such women, selfish, sweet, false, that entice fools.

Gautami. You have no right to say that. She grew up in the pious grove. She does not know how to deceive.

King. Old hermit woman,

The female's untaught cunning may be seen
In beasts, far more in women selfish-wise;
The cuckoo's eggs are left to hatch and rear
By foster-parents, and away she flies.

Shakuntala (*angrily*). Wretch! You judge all this by your own false heart. Would any other man do what you have done? To hide behind virtue, like a yawning well covered over with grass!

King (*to himself*). But her anger is free from coquetry, because she has lived in the forest. See!

Her glance is straight; her eyes are flashing red;
Her speech is harsh, not drawlingly well-bred;
Her whole lip quivers, seems to shake with cold;
Her frown has straightened eyebrows arching bold.

No, she saw that I was doubtful, and her anger was feigned. Thus

When I refused but now
Hard-heartedly, to know
Of love or secret vow,
Her eyes grew red; and so,
Bending her arching brow,
She fiercely snapped Love's bow.

(*Aloud.*) My good girl, Dushyanta's conduct is known to the whole kingdom, but not this action.

Shakuntala. Well, well. I had my way. I trusted a king, and put myself in his hands. He had a honey face and a heart of stone. (*She covers her face with her dress and weeps.*)

Sharngarava. Thus does unbridled levity burn.

Be slow to love, but yet more slow
With secret mate;
With those whose hearts we do not know,
Love turns to hate.

King. Why do you trust this girl, and accuse me of an imaginary crime? *Sharngarava* (*disdainfully*). You have learned your wisdom upside down.

It would be monstrous to believe
A girl who never lies;
Trust those who study to deceive
And think it very wise.

King. Aha, my candid friend! Suppose I were to admit that I am such a man. What would happen if I deceived the girl?

Sharngarava. Ruin.

King. It is unthinkable that ruin should fall on Puru's line.

Sharngarava. Why bandy words? We have fulfilled our Father's bidding. We are ready to return.

Leave her or take her, as you will;
She is your wife;
Husbands have power for good or ill
O'er woman's life.

Gautami, lead the way. (*They start to go.*)

Shakuntala. He has deceived me shamelessly. And will you leave me too? (*She starts to follow.*)

Gautami (*turns around and sees her*). Sharngarava, my son, Shakuntala is following us, lamenting piteously. What can the poor child do with a husband base enough to reject her?

Sharngarava (*turns angrily*). You self-willed girl! Do you dare show independence? (SHAKUNTALA *shrinks in fear.*) Listen.

If you deserve such scorn and blame,
What will your father with your shame?
But if you know your vows are pure,
Obey your husband and endure.

Remain. We must go.

King. Hermit, why deceive this woman? Remember:

Night-blossoms open to the moon,
Day-blossoms to the sun;
A man of honour ever strives
Another's wife to shun.

Sharngarava. O King, suppose you had forgotten your former actions in the midst of distractions. Should you now desert your wife—you who fear to fail in virtue?

King. I ask *you* which is the heavier sin:

Not knowing whether I be mad
Or falsehood be in her,
Shall I desert a faithful wife
Or turn adulterer?

Chaplain (*considering*). Now if this were done—

King. Instruct me, my teacher.

Chaplain. Let the woman remain in my house until her child is born.

King. Why this?

Chaplain. The chief astrologers have told you that your first child was destined to be an emperor. If the son of the hermit's daughter is born with the imperial birthmarks, then welcome her and introduce her into the palace. Otherwise, she must return to her father.

King. It is good advice, my teacher.

Chaplain (*rising*). Follow me, my daughter.

Shakuntala. O mother earth, give me a grave! (*Exit weeping, with the chaplain, the hermits, and* GAUTAMI. *The king, his memory clouded by the curse, ponders on* SHAKUNTALA.)

Voices behind the scenes. A miracle! A miracle!

King (*listening*). What does this mean? (*Enter the chaplain*.)

Chaplain (*in amazement*). Your Majesty, a wonderful thing has happened.

King. What?

Chaplain. When Kanva's pupils had departed,

She tossed her arms, bemoaned her plight,
Accused her crushing fate—

King. What then?

Chaplain.

Before our eyes a heavenly light
In woman's form, but shining bright,
Seized her and vanished straight.

(*All betray astonishment*.)

King. My teacher, we have already settled the matter. Why speculate in vain? Let us seek repose. *Chaplain*. Victory to your Majesty. (*Exit*.)

King. Vetravati, I am bewildered. Conduct me to my apartment.

Portress. Follow me, your Majesty.

King (*walks about. To himself*).

With a hermit-wife I had no part,
All memories evade me;
And yet my sad and stricken heart
Would more than half persuade me.

(*Exeunt omnes*.)

ACT VI
SEPARATION FROM SHAKUNTALA

SCENE I.—*In the street before the Palace*

(*Enter the chief of police, two policemen, and a man with his hands bound behind his back.*)

The two policemen (*striking the man*). Now, pickpocket, tell us where you found this ring. It is the king's ring, with letters engraved on it, and it has a magnificent great gem.

Fisherman (*showing fright*). Be merciful, kind gentlemen. I am not guilty of such a crime.

First policeman. No, I suppose the king thought you were a pious Brahman, and made you a present of it.

Fisherman. Listen, please. I am a fisherman, and I live on the Ganges, at the spot where Indra came down.

Second policeman. You thief, we didn't ask for your address or your social position.

Chief. Let him tell a straight story, Suchaka. Don't interrupt.

The two policemen. Yes, chief. Talk, man, talk.

Fisherman. I support my family with things you catch fish with—nets, you know, and hooks, and things.

Chief (*laughing*). You have a sweet trade.

Fisherman. Don't say that, master.

You can't give up a lowdown trade
That your ancestors began;
A butcher butchers things, and yet
He's the tenderest-hearted man.

Chief. Go on. Go on.

Fisherman. Well, one day I was cutting up a carp. In its maw I see this ring with the magnificent great gem. And then I was just trying to sell it here when you kind gentlemen grabbed me. That is the only way I got it. Now kill me, or find fault with me.

Chief (*smelling the ring*). There is no doubt about it, Januka. It has been in a fish's maw. It has the real perfume of raw meat. Now we have to find out how he got it. We must go to the palace.

The two policemen (*to the fisherman*). Move on, you cutpurse, move on. (*They walk about.*)

Chief. Suchaka, wait here at the big gate until I come out of the palace. And don't get careless.

The two policemen. Go in, chief. I hope the king will be nice to you.

Chief. Good-bye. (*Exit.*)

Suchaka. Januka, the chief is taking his time.

Januka. You can't just drop in on a king.

Suchaka. Januka, my fingers are itching (*indicating the fisherman*) to kill this cutpurse.

Fisherman. Don't kill a man without any reason, master.

Januka (*looking ahead*). There is the chief, with a written order from the king. (*To the fisherman.*) Now you will see your family, or else you will feed the crows and jackals. (*Enter the chief.*)

Chief. Quick! Quick! (*He breaks off.*)

Fisherman. Oh, oh! I'm a dead man. (*He shows dejection.*)

Chief. Release him, you. Release the fishnet fellow. It is all right, his getting the ring. Our king told me so himself.

Suchaka. All right, chief. He is a dead man come back to life. (*He releases the fisherman.*)

Fisherman (*bowing low to the chief*). Master, I owe you my life. (*He falls at his feet.*)

Chief. Get up, get up! Here is a reward that the king was kind enough to give you. It is worth as much as the ring. Take it. (*He hands the fisherman a bracelet.*)

Fisherman (*joyfully taking it*). Much obliged.

Januka. He *is* much obliged to the king. Just as if he had been taken from the stake and put on an elephant's back.

Suchaka. Chief, the reward shows that the king thought a lot of the ring. The gem must be worth something.

Chief. No, it wasn't the fine gem that pleased the king. It was this way.

The two policemen. Well?

Chief. I think, when the king saw it, he remembered somebody he loves. You know how dignified he is usually. But as soon as he saw it, he broke down for a moment.

Suchaka. You have done the king a good turn, chief.

Januka. All for the sake of this fish-killer, it seems to me. (*He looks enviously at the fisherman.*)

Fisherman. Take half of it, masters, to pay for something to drink.

Januka. Fisherman, you are the biggest and best friend I've got. The first thing we want, is all the brandy we can hold. Let's go where they keep it. (*Exeunt omnes.*)

SCENE II.—*In the Palace Gardens*

(*Enter* MISHRAKESHI, *flying through the air.*)

Mishrakeshi. I have taken my turn in waiting upon the nymphs. And now I will see what this good king is doing. Shakuntala is like a second self to me, because she is the daughter of Menaka. And it was she who asked me to do this. (*She looks about.*) It is the day of the spring festival. But I see no preparations for a celebration at court. I might learn the reason by my power of divination. But I must do as my friend asked me. Good! I will make myself invisible and stand near these girls who take care of the garden. I shall find out that way. (*She descends to earth. Enter a maid, gazing at a mango branch, and behind her, a second.*)

First maid.

First mango-twig, so pink, so green,
First living breath of spring,
You are sacrificed as soon as seen,
A festival offering.

Second maid. What are you chirping about to yourself, little cuckoo?

First maid. Why, little bee, you know that the cuckoo goes crazy with delight when she sees the mango-blossom.

Second maid (*joyfully*). Oh, has the spring really come?

First maid. Yes, little bee. And this is the time when you too buzz about in crazy joy. *Second maid.* Hold me, dear, while I stand on tiptoe and offer this blossom to Love, the divine.

First maid. If I do, you must give me half the reward of the offering.

Second maid. That goes without saying, dear. We two are one. (*She leans on her friend and takes the mango-blossom.*) Oh, see! The mango-blossom hasn't opened, but it has broken the sheath, so it is fragrant. (*She brings her hands together.*) I worship mighty Love.

O mango-twig I give to Love
As arrow for his bow,
Most sovereign of his arrows five,
Strike maiden-targets low.

(*She throws the twig. Enter the chamberlain.*)

Chamberlain (*angrily*). Stop, silly girl. The king has strictly forbidden the spring festival. Do you dare pluck the mango-blossoms?

The two maids (*frightened*). Forgive us, sir. We did not know.

Chamberlain. What! You have not heard the king's command, which is obeyed even by the trees of spring and the creatures that dwell in them. See!

The mango branches are in bloom,
Yet pollen does not form;
The cuckoo's song sticks in his throat,
Although the days are warm;

The amaranth-bud is formed, and yet
Its power of growth is gone;
The love-god timidly puts by
The arrow he has drawn.

Mishrakeshi. There is no doubt of it. This good king has wonderful power.

First maid. A few days ago, sir, we were sent to his Majesty by his brother-in-law Mitravasu to decorate the garden. That is why we have heard nothing of this affair.

Chamberlain. You must not do so again.

The two maids. But we are curious. If we girls may know about it, pray tell us, sir. Why did his Majesty forbid the spring festival?

Mishrakeshi. Kings are fond of celebrations. There must be some good reason.

Chamberlain (*to himself*). It is in everybody's mouth. Why should I not tell it? (*Aloud*.) Have you heard the gossip concerning Shakuntala's rejection?

The two maids. Yes, sir. The king's brother-in-law told us, up to the point where the ring was recovered.

Chamberlain. There is little more to tell. When his Majesty saw the ring, he remembered that he had indeed contracted a secret marriage with Shakuntala, and had rejected her under a delusion. And then he fell a prey to remorse.

He hates the things he loved; he intermits
The daily audience, nor in judgment sits;
Spends sleepless nights in tossing on his bed;
At times, when he by courtesy is led
To address a lady, speaks another name,
Then stands for minutes, sunk in helpless shame.

Mishrakeshi. I am glad to hear it.

Chamberlain. His Majesty's sorrow has forbidden the festival.

The two maids. It is only right.

A voice behind the scenes. Follow me.

Chamberlain (*listening*). Ah, his Majesty approaches. Go, and attend to your duties. (*Exeunt the two maids. Enter the king, wearing a dress indicative of remorse; the clown, and the portress.*)

Chamberlain (*observing the king*). A beautiful figure charms in whatever state. Thus, his Majesty is pleasing even in his sorrow. For

All ornament is laid aside; he wears
One golden bracelet on his wasted arm;
His lip is scorched by sighs; and sleepless cares
Redden his eyes. Yet all can work no harm
On that magnificent beauty, wasting, but
Gaining in brilliance, like a diamond cut.

Mishrakeshi (*observing the king*). No wonder Shakuntala pines for him, even though he dishonoured her by his rejection of her.

King (*walks about slowly, sunk in thought*).

Alas! My smitten heart, that once lay sleeping,
Heard in its dreams my fawn-eyed love's laments,
And wakened now, awakens but to weeping,
To bitter grief, and tears of penitence.

Mishrakeshi. That is the poor girl's fate.

Clown (*to himself*). He has got his Shakuntala-sickness again. I wish I knew how to cure him.

Chamberlain (advancing). Victory to your Majesty. I have examined the garden. Your Majesty may visit its retreats.

King. Vetravati, tell the minister Pishuna in my name that a sleepless night prevents me from mounting the throne of judgment. He is to investigate the citizens' business and send me a memorandum.

Portress. Yes, your Majesty. *(Exit.)*

King. And you, Parvatayana, return to your post of duty.

Chamberlain. Yes, your Majesty. (*Exit*.)

Clown. You have got rid of the vermin. Now amuse yourself in this garden. It is delightful with the passing of the cold weather.

King (*sighing*). My friend, the proverb makes no mistake. Misfortune finds the weak spot. See!

No sooner did the darkness lift
That clouded memory's power,
Than the god of love prepared his bow
And shot the mango-flower.

No sooner did the ring recall
My banished maiden dear,
No sooner do I vainly weep
For her, than spring is here.

Clown. Wait a minute, man. I will destroy Love's arrow with my stick. (*He raises his stick and strikes at the mango branch.*)

King (*smiling*). Enough! I see your pious power. My friend, where shall I sit now to comfort my eyes with the vines? They remind me somehow of her.

Clown. Well, you told one of the maids, the clever painter, that you would spend this hour in the bower of spring-creepers. And you asked her to bring you there the picture of the lady Shakuntala which you painted on a tablet.

King. It is my only consolation. Lead the way to the bower of spring-creepers.

Clown. Follow me. (*They walk about.* MISHRAKESHI *follows.*) Here is the bower of spring-creepers, with its jewelled benches. Its loneliness seems to bid you a silent welcome. Let us go in and sit down. (*They do so.*)

Mishrakeshi. I will hide among the vines and see the dear girl's picture. Then I shall be able to tell her how deep her husband's love is. (*She hides.*)

King (*sighing*). I remember it all now, my friend. I told you how I first met Shakuntala. It is true, you were not with me when I rejected her. But I had told you of her at the first. Had you forgotten, as I did?

Mishrakeshi. This shows that a king should not be separated a single moment from some intimate friend.

Clown. No, I didn't forget. But when you had told the whole story, you said it was a joke and there was nothing in it. And I was fool enough to believe you. No, this is the work of fate.

Mishrakeshi. It must be.

King (*after meditating a moment*). Help me, my friend.

Clown. But, man, this isn't right at all. A good man never lets grief get the upper hand. The mountains are calm even in a tempest.

King. My friend, I am quite forlorn. I keep thinking of her pitiful state when I rejected her. Thus:

When I denied her, then she tried
To join her people. "Stay," one cried,
Her father's representative.
She stopped, she turned, she could but give
A tear-dimmed glance to heartless me—
That arrow burns me poisonously.

Mishrakeshi. How his fault distresses him!

Clown. Well, I don't doubt it was some heavenly being that carried her away.

King. Who else would dare to touch a faithful wife? Her friends told me that Menaka was her mother. My heart persuades me that it was she, or companions of hers, who carried Shakuntala away.

Mishrakeshi. His madness was wonderful, not his awakening reason.

Clown. But in that case, you ought to take heart. You will meet her again.

King. How so?

Clown. Why, a mother or a father cannot long bear to see a daughter separated from her husband.

King. My friend,

And was it phantom, madness, dream,
Or fatal retribution stern?
My hopes fell down a precipice
And never, never will return.

Clown. Don't talk that way. Why, the ring shows that incredible meetings do happen.

King (*looking at the ring*). This ring deserves pity. It has fallen from a heaven hard to earn.

Your virtue, ring, like mine,
Is proved to be but small;

Her pink-nailed finger sweet
You clasped. How could you fall?

Mishrakeshi. If it were worn on any other hand, it would deserve pity. My dear girl, you are far away. I am the only one to hear these delightful words.

Clown. Tell me how you put the ring on her finger.

Mishrakeshi. He speaks as if prompted by my curiosity.

King. Listen, my friend. When I left the pious grove for the city, my darling wept and said: "But how long will you remember us, dear?"

Clown. And then you said—--

King. Then I put this engraved ring on her finger, and said to her—--

Clown. Well, what?

King.

Count every day one letter of my name;
Before you reach the end, dear,
Will come to lead you to my palace halls
A guide whom I shall send, dear.

Then, through my madness, it fell out cruelly. *Mishrakeshi.* It was too charming an agreement to be frustrated by fate.

Clown. But how did it get into a carp's mouth, as if it had been a fish-hook?

King. While she was worshipping the Ganges at Shachitirtha, it fell.

Clown. I see.

Mishrakeshi. That is why the virtuous king doubted his marriage with poor Shakuntala. Yet such love does not ask for a token. How could it have been?

King. Well, I can only reproach this ring.

Clown (*smiling*). And I will reproach this stick of mine. Why are you crooked when I am straight?

King (*not hearing him*).

How could you fail to linger
On her soft, tapering finger,
And in the water fall?

And yet

Things lifeless know not beauty;
But I—I scorned my duty,
The sweetest task of all.

Mishrakeshi. He has given the answer which I had ready.

Clown. But that is no reason why I should starve to death.

King (*not heeding*). O my darling, my heart burns with repentance because I abandoned you without reason. Take pity on me. Let me see you again. (*Enter a maid with a tablet.*)

Maid. Your Majesty, here is the picture of our lady. (*She produces the tablet.*)

King (*gazing at it*). It is a beautiful picture. See!

A graceful arch of brows above great eyes;
Lips bathed in darting, smiling light that flies
Reflected from white teeth; a mouth as red
As red karkandhu-fruit; love's brightness shed
O'er all her face in bursts of liquid charm—
The picture speaks, with living beauty warm.

Clown (*looking at it*). The sketch is full of sweet meaning. My eyes seem to stumble over its uneven surface. What more can I say? I expect to see it come to life, and I feel like speaking to it.

Mishrakeshi. The king is a clever painter. I seem to see the dear girl before me.

King. My friend,

What in the picture is not fair,
Is badly done;
Yet something of her beauty there,
I feel, is won.

Mishrakeshi. This is natural, when love is increased by remorse.

King (*sighing*).

I treated her with scorn and loathing ever;
Now o'er her pictured charms my heart will burst:
A traveller I, who scorned the mighty river.
And seeks in the mirage to quench his thirst.

Clown. There are three figures in the picture, and they are all beautiful. Which one is the lady Shakuntala?

Mishrakeshi. The poor fellow never saw her beauty. His eyes are useless, for she never came before them.

King. Which one do you think?

Clown (*observing closely*). I think it is this one, leaning against the creeper which she has just sprinkled. Her face is hot and the flowers are dropping from her hair; for the ribbon is loosened. Her arms droop like weary branches; she has loosened her girdle, and she seems a little fatigued. This, I think, is the lady Shakuntala, the others are her friends.

King. You are good at guessing. Besides, here are proofs of my love.

See where discolorations faint
Of loving handling tell;
And here the swelling of the paint
Shows where my sad tears fell.

Chaturika, I have not finished the background. Go, get the brushes.

Maid. Please hold the picture, Madhavya, while I am gone.

King. I will hold it. (*He does so. Exit maid.*)

Clown. What are you going to add?

Mishrakeshi. Surely, every spot that the dear girl loved.

King. Listen, my friend.

The stream of Malini, and on its sands
The swan-pairs resting; holy foot-hill lands
Of great Himalaya's sacred ranges, where
The yaks are seen; and under trees that bear
Bark hermit-dresses on their branches high,
A doe that on the buck's horn rubs her eye.

Clown (*aside*). To hear him talk, I should think he was going to fill up the picture with heavy-bearded hermits.

King. And another ornament that Shakuntala loved I have forgotten to paint.

Clown. What?

Mishrakeshi. Something natural for a girl living in the forest.

King.

The siris-blossom, fastened o'er her ear,
Whose stamens brush her cheek;
The lotus-chain like autumn moonlight soft
Upon her bosom meek.

Clown. But why does she cover her face with fingers lovely as the pink water-lily? She seems frightened. (*He looks more closely.*) I see. Here is a bold, bad bee. He steals honey, and so he flies to her lotus-face.

King. Drive him away.

Clown. It is your affair to punish evil-doers.

King. True. O welcome guest of the flowering vine, why do you waste your time in buzzing here?

Your faithful, loving queen,
Perched on a flower, athirst,
Is waiting for you still,
Nor tastes the honey first.

Mishrakeshi. A gentlemanly way to drive him off!

Clown. This kind are obstinate, even when you warn them.

King (*angrily*). Will you not obey my command? Then listen:

'Tis sweet as virgin blossoms on a tree,
The lip I kissed in love-feasts tenderly;
Sting that dear lip, O bee, with cruel power,
And you shall be imprisoned in a flower.

Clown. Well, he doesn't seem afraid of your dreadful punishment. (*Laughing. To himself*.) The man is crazy, and I am just as bad, from associating with him.

King. Will he not go, though I warn him?

Mishrakeshi. Love works a curious change even in a brave man.

Clown (*aloud*). It is only a picture, man.

King. A picture?

Mishrakeshi. I too understand it now. But to him, thoughts are real experiences.

King. You have done an ill-natured thing.

When I was happy in the sight,
And when my heart was warm,
You brought sad memories back, and made
My love a painted form.

(*He sheds a tear*.)

Mishrakeshi. Fate plays strangely with him.

King. My friend, how can I endure a grief that has no respite?

I cannot sleep at night
And meet her dreaming;
I cannot see the sketch
While tears are streaming.

Mishrakeshi. My friend, you have indeed atoned—and in her friend's presence—for the pain you caused by rejecting dear Shakuntala. (*Enter the maid* CHATURIKA.)

Maid. Your Majesty, I was coming back with the box of paint-brushes—

King. Well?

Maid. I met Queen Vasumati with the maid Pingalika. And the queen snatched the box from me, saying: "I will take it to the king myself."

Clown. How did you escape?

Maid. The queen's dress caught on a vine. And while her maid was setting her free, I excused myself in a hurry. *A voice behind the scenes*. Follow me, your Majesty.

Clown (*listening*). Man, the she-tiger of the palace is making a spring on her prey. She means to make one mouthful of the maid.

King. My friend, the queen has come because she feels touched in her honour. You had better take care of this picture.

Clown. "And yourself," you might add. (*He takes the picture and rises.*) If you get out of the trap alive, call for me at the Cloud Balcony. And I will hide the thing there so that nothing but a pigeon could find it. (*Exit on the run.*)

Mishrakeshi. Though his heart is given to another, he is courteous to his early flame. He is a constant friend.

(*Enter the portress with a document.*)

Portress. Victory to your Majesty.

King. Vetravati, did you not meet Queen Vasumati?

Portress. Yes, your Majesty. But she turned back when she saw that I carried a document.

King. The queen knows times and seasons. She will not interrupt business.

Portress. Your Majesty, the minister sends word that in the press of various business he has attended to only one citizen's suit. This he has reduced to writing for your Majesty's perusal.

King. Give me the document. (*The portress does so.*)

King (*reads*). "Be it known to his Majesty. A seafaring merchant named Dhanavriddhi has been lost in a shipwreck. He is childless, and his property, amounting to several millions, reverts to the crown. Will his Majesty take action?" (*Sadly.*) It is dreadful to be childless. Vetravati, he had great riches. There must be several wives. Let inquiry be made. There may be a wife who is with child.

Portress. We have this moment heard that a merchant's daughter of Saketa is his wife. And she is soon to become a mother.

King. The child shall receive the inheritance. Go, inform the minister.

Portress. Yes, your Majesty. (*She starts to go.*)

King. Wait a moment.

Portress (*turning back*). Yes, your Majesty. *King.* After all, what does it matter whether he have issue or not?

Let King Dushyanta be proclaimed
To every sad soul kin
That mourns a kinsman loved and lost,
Yet did not plunge in sin.

Portress. The proclamation shall be made. (*She goes out and soon returns.*) Your Majesty, the royal proclamation was welcomed by the populace as is a timely shower.

King (*sighing deeply*). Thus, when issue fails, wealth passes, on the death of the head of the family, to a stranger. When I die, it will be so with the glory of Puru's line.

Portress. Heaven avert the omen!

King. Alas! I despised the happiness that offered itself to me.

Mishrakeshi. Without doubt, he has dear Shakuntala in mind when he thus reproaches himself.

King.

Could I forsake the virtuous wife
Who held my best, my future life
And cherished it for glorious birth,
As does the seed-receiving earth?

Mishrakeshi. She will not long be forsaken.

Maid (*to the portress*). Mistress, the minister's report has doubled our lord's remorse. Go to the Cloud Balcony and bring Madhavya to dispel his grief.

Portress. A good suggestion. (*Exit.*)

King. Alas! The ancestors of Dushyanta are in a doubtful case.

For I am childless, and they do not know,
When I am gone, what child of theirs will bring
The scriptural oblation; and their tears
Already mingle with my offering.

Mishrakeshi. He is screened from the light, and is in darkness.

Maid. Do not give way to grief, your Majesty. You are in the prime of your years, and the birth of a son to one of your other wives will make you blameless before your ancestors. (*To herself.*) He does not heed me. The proper medicine is needed for any disease.

King (*betraying his sorrow*). Surely,

The royal line that flowed
A river pure and grand,

Dies in the childless king,
Like streams in desert sand.

(*He swoons.*)

Maid (*in distress*). Oh, sir, come to yourself.

Mishrakeski. Shall I make him happy now? No, I heard the mother of the gods consoling Shakuntala. She said that the gods, impatient for the sacrifice, would soon cause him to welcome his true wife. I must delay no longer. I will comfort dear Shakuntala with my tidings. (*Exit through the air.*)

A voice behind the scenes. Help, help!

King (*comes to himself and listens*). It sounds as if Madhavya were in distress.

Maid. Your Majesty, I hope that Pingalika and the other maids did not catch poor Madhavya with the picture in his hands.

King. Go, Chaturika. Reprove the queen in my name for not controlling her servants.

Maid. Yes, your Majesty. (*Exit.*)

The voice. Help, help!

King. The Brahman's voice seems really changed by fear. Who waits without? (*Enter the chamberlain.*)

Chamberlain. Your Majesty commands?

King. See why poor Madhavya is screaming so.

Chamberlain. I will see. (*He goes out, and returns trembling.*)

King. Parvatayana, I hope it is nothing very dreadful.

Chamberlain. I hope not.

King. Then why do you tremble so? For

Why should the trembling, born
Of age, increasing, seize
Your limbs and bid them shake
Like fig-leaves in the breeze?

Chamberlain. Save your friend, O King!

King. From what?

Chamberlain. From great danger.

King. Speak plainly, man.

Chamberlain. On the Cloud Balcony, open to the four winds of heaven—--

King. What has happened there?

Chamberlain.

While he was resting on its height,
Which palace peacocks in their flight
Can hardly reach, he seemed to be
Snatched up—by what, we could not see.

King (*rising quickly*). My very palace is invaded by evil creatures. To be a king, is to be a disappointed man.

The moral stumblings of mine own,
The daily slips, are scarcely known;
Who then that rules a kingdom, can
Guide every deed of every man?

The voice. Hurry, hurry!

King (*hears the voice and quickens his steps*). Have no fear, my friend.

The voice. Have no fear! When something has got me by the back of the neck, and is trying to break my bones like a piece of sugar-cane!

King (*looks about*). A bow! a bow! (*Enter a Greek woman with a bow.*)

Greek woman. A bow and arrows, your Majesty. And here are the finger-guards. (*The king takes the bow and arrows.*)

Another voice behind the scenes.

Writhe, while I drink the red blood flowing clear
And kill you, as a tiger kills a deer;
Let King Dushyanta grasp his bow; but how
Can all his kingly valour save you now?

King (*angrily*). He scorns me, too! In one moment, miserable demon, you shall die. (*Stringing his bow.*) Where is the stairway, Parvatayana?

Chamberlain. Here, your Majesty. (*All make haste.*)

King (*Looking about*). There is no one here.

The Clown's voice. Save me, save me! I see you, if you can't see me. I am a mouse in the claws of the cat. I am done for. *King*. You are proud of your invisibility. But shall not my arrow see you? Stand still. Do not hope to escape by clinging to my friend.

My arrow, flying when the bow is bent,
Shall slay the wretch and spare the innocent;
When milk is mixed with water in a cup,
Swans leave the water, and the milk drink up.

(*He takes aim. Enter* MATALI *and the clown.*)

Matali. O King, as Indra, king of the gods, commands,

Seek foes among the evil powers alone;
For them your bow should bend;
Not cruel shafts, but glances soft and kind
Should fall upon a friend.

King (*hastily withdrawing the arrow*). It is Matali. Welcome to the charioteer of heaven's king.

Clown. Well! He came within an inch of butchering me. And you welcome him.

Matali (*smiling*). Hear, O King, for what purpose Indra sends me to you.

King. I am all attention.

Matali. There is a host of demons who call themselves Invincible—the brood of Kalanemi.

King. So Narada has told me.

Matali.

Heaven's king is powerless; you shall smite
His foes in battle soon;
Darkness that overcomes the day,
Is scattered by the moon.

Take your bow at once, enter my heavenly chariot, and set forth for victory.

King. I am grateful for the honour which Indra shows me. But why did you act thus toward Madhavya?

Matali. I will tell you. I saw that you were overpowered by some inner sorrow, and acted thus to rouse you. For

The spurnèd snake will swell his hood;
Fire blazes when 'tis stirred;
Brave men are roused to fighting mood
By some insulting word.

King. Friend Madhavya, I must obey the bidding of heaven's king. Go, acquaint the minister Pishuna with the matter, and add these words of mine:

Your wisdom only shall control
The kingdom for a time;
My bow is strung; a distant goal
Calls me, and tasks sublime.

Clown. Very well. (*Exit*.)

Matali. Enter the chariot. (*The king does so. Exeunt omnes.*)

ACT VII

(*Enter, in a chariot that flies through the air, the king and* MATALI.)

King. Matali, though I have done what Indra commanded, I think myself an unprofitable servant, when I remember his most gracious welcome.

Matali. O King, know that each considers himself the other's debtor. For

You count the service given
Small by the welcome paid,
Which to the king of heaven
Seems mean for such brave aid.

King. Ah, no! For the honour given me at parting went far beyond imagination. Before the gods, he seated me beside him on his throne. And then

He smiled, because his son Jayanta's heart
Beat quicker, by the self-same wish oppressed,
And placed about my neck the heavenly wreath
Still fragrant from the sandal on his breast.

Matali. But what do you not deserve from heaven's king? Remember:

Twice, from peace-loving Indra's sway
The demon-thorn was plucked away:
First, by Man-lion's crooked claws;
Again, by your smooth shafts to-day.

King. This merely proves Indra's majesty. Remember:

All servants owe success in enterprise
To honour paid before the great deed's done;
Could dawn defeat the darkness otherwise
Than resting on the chariot of the sun?

Matali. The feeling becomes you. (*After a little.*) See, O King! Your glory has the happiness of being published abroad in heaven.

With colours used by nymphs of heaven
To make their beauty shine,
Gods write upon the surface given
Of many a magic vine,
As worth their song, the simple story
Of those brave deeds that made your glory.

King. Matali, when I passed before, I was intent on fighting the demons, and did not observe this region. Tell me. In which path of the winds are we?

Matali.

It is the windpath sanctified
By holy Vishnu's second stride;
Which, freed from dust of passion, ever
Upholds the threefold heavenly river;
And, driving them with reins of light,
Guides the stars in wheeling flight.

King. That is why serenity pervades me, body and soul. (*He observes the path taken by the chariot.*) It seems that we have descended into the region of the clouds.

Matali. How do you perceive it?

King.

Plovers that fly from mountain-caves,
Steeds that quick-flashing lightning laves,
And chariot-wheels that drip with spray—
A path o'er pregnant clouds betray.

Matali. You are right. And in a moment you will be in the world over which you bear rule.

King (*looking down*). Matali, our quick descent gives the world of men a mysterious look. For

The plains appear to melt and fall
From mountain peaks that grow more tall;
The trunks of trees no longer hide
Nor in their leafy nests abide;
The river network now is clear,
For smaller streams at last appear:
It seems as if some being threw
The world to me, for clearer view.

Matali. You are a good observer, O King. (*He looks down, awe-struck.*) There is a noble loveliness in the earth. *King.* Matali, what mountain is this, its flanks sinking into the eastern and into the western sea? It drips liquid gold like a cloud at sunset.

Matali. O King, this is Gold Peak, the mountain of the fairy centaurs. Here it is that ascetics most fully attain to magic powers. See!

The ancient sage, Marichi's son,
Child of the Uncreated One,
Father of superhuman life,
Dwells here austerely with his wife.

King (*reverently*). I must not neglect the happy chance. I cannot go farther until I have walked humbly about the holy one.

Matali. It is a worthy thought, O King. (*The chariot descends*.) We have come down to earth.

King (*astonished*). Matali,

The wheels are mute on whirling rim;
Unstirred, the dust is lying there;
We do not bump the earth, but skim:
Still, still we seem to fly through air.

Matali. Such is the glory of the chariot which obeys you and Indra.

King. In which direction lies the hermitage of Marichi's son?

Matali (*pointing*). See!

Where stands the hermit, horridly austere,
Whom clinging vines are choking, tough and sore;
Half-buried in an ant-hill that has grown
About him, standing post-like and alone;
Sun-staring with dim eyes that know no rest,
The dead skin of a serpent on his breast:
So long he stood unmoved, insensate there
That birds build nests within his mat of hair.

King (*gazing*). All honour to one who mortifies the flesh so terribly.

Matali (*checking the chariot*). We have entered the hermitage of the ancient sage, whose wife Aditi tends the coral-trees. *King*. Here is deeper contentment than in heaven. I seem plunged in a pool of nectar.

Matali (*stopping the chariot*). Descend, O King.

King (*descending*). But how will you fare?

Matali. The chariot obeys the word of command. I too will descend. (*He does so*.) Before you, O King, are the groves where the holiest hermits lead their self-denying life.

King. I look with amazement both at their simplicity and at what they might enjoy.

Their appetites are fed with air
Where grows whatever is most fair;
They bathe religiously in pools
Which golden lily-pollen cools;
They pray within a jewelled home,
Are chaste where nymphs of heaven roam:
They mortify desire and sin
With things that others fast to win.

Matali. The desires of the great aspire high. (*He walks about and speaks to some one not visible.*) Ancient Shakalya, how is Marichi's holy son occupied? (*He listens.*) What do you say? That he is explaining to Aditi, in answer to her question, the duties of a faithful wife? My matter must await a fitter time. (*He turns to the king.*) Wait here, O King, in the shade of the ashoka tree, till I have announced your coming to the sire of Indra.

King. Very well. (*Exit* MATALI. *The king's arm throbs, a happy omen.*)

I dare not hope for what I pray;
Why thrill—in vain?
For heavenly bliss once thrown away
Turns into pain.

A voice behind the scenes. Don't! You mustn't be so foolhardy. Oh, you are always the same.

King (*listening*). No naughtiness could feel at home in this spot. Who draws such a rebuke upon himself? (*He looks towards the sound. In surprise.*) It is a child, but no child in strength. And two hermit-women are trying to control him.

He drags a struggling lion cub,
The lioness' milk half-sucked, half-missed,
Towzles his mane, and tries to drub
Him tame with small, imperious fist.

(*Enter a small boy, as described, and two hermit-women.*)

Boy. Open your mouth, cub. I want to count your teeth.

First woman. Naughty boy, why do you torment our pets? They are like children to us. Your energy seems to take the form of striking something. No wonder the hermits call you All-tamer.

King. Why should my heart go out to this boy as if he were my own son? (*He reflects.*) No doubt my childless state makes me sentimental.

Second woman. The lioness will spring at you if you don't let her baby go.

Boy (*smiling*). Oh, I'm dreadfully scared. (*He bites his lip.*)

King (*in surprise*).

The boy is seed of fire
Which, when it grows, will burn;
A tiny spark that soon
To awful flame may turn.

First woman. Let the little lion go, dear. I will give you another plaything.

Boy. Where is it? Give it to me. (*He stretches out his hand.*)

King (*looking at the hand.*) He has one of the imperial birthmarks! For

Between the eager fingers grow
The close-knit webs together drawn,
Like some lone lily opening slow
To meet the kindling blush of dawn.

Second woman. Suvrata, we can't make him stop by talking. Go. In my cottage you will find a painted clay peacock that belongs to the hermit-boy Mankanaka. Bring him that.

First woman. I will. (*Exit*.) *Boy*. Meanwhile I'll play with this one.

Hermit-woman (*looks and laughs*). Let him go.

King. My heart goes out to this wilful child. (*Sighing*.)

They show their little buds of teeth
In peals of causeless laughter;
They hide their trustful heads beneath
Your heart. And stumbling after
Come sweet, unmeaning sounds that sing
To you. The father warms
And loves the very dirt they bring
Upon their little forms.

Hermit-woman (*shaking her finger*). Won't you mind me? (*She looks about*.) Which one of the hermit-boys is here? (*She sees the king*.) Oh, sir, please come here and free this lion cub. The little rascal is tormenting him, and I can't make him let go.

King. Very well. (*He approaches, smiling*.) O little son of a great sage!

Your conduct in this place apart,
Is most unfit
'Twould grieve your father's pious heart
And trouble it.

To animals he is as good
As good can be;
You spoil it, like a black snake's brood
In sandal tree.

Hermit-woman. But, sir, he is not the son of a hermit.

King. So it would seem, both from his looks and his actions. But in this spot, I had no suspicion of anything else. (*He loosens the boy's hold on the cub, and touching him, says to himself.*)

It makes me thrill to touch the boy,
The stranger's son, to me unknown;
What measureless content must fill
The man who calls the child his own!

Hermit-woman (*looking at the two*). Wonderful! wonderful!

King. Why do you say that, mother? *Hermit-woman*. I am astonished to see how much the boy looks like you, sir. You are not related. Besides, he is a perverse little creature and he does not know you. Yet he takes no dislike to you.

King (*caressing the boy*). Mother, if he is not the son of a hermit, what is his family?

Hermit-woman. The family of Puru.

King (*to himself*). He is of one family with me! Then could my thought be true? (*Aloud.*) But this is the custom of Puru's line:

In glittering palaces they dwell
While men, and rule the country well;
Then make the grove their home in age,
And die in austere hermitage.

But how could human beings, of their own mere motion, attain this spot?

Hermit-woman. You are quite right, sir. But the boy's mother was related to a nymph, and she bore her son in the pious grove of the father of the gods.

King (*to himself*). Ah, a second ground for hope. (*Aloud.*) What was the name of the good king whose wife she was?

Hermit-woman. Who would speak his name? He rejected his true wife.

King (to himself). This story points at me. Suppose I ask the boy for his mother's name. (*He reflects.*) No, it is wrong to concern myself with one who may be another's wife.

(*Enter the first woman, with the clay peacock.*)

First woman. Look, All-tamer. Here is the bird, the *shakunta.* Isn't the *shakunta* lovely?

Boy (looks about). Where is my mamma? (*The two women burst out laughing.*)

First woman. It sounded like her name, and deceived him. He loves his mother.

Second woman. She said: "See how pretty the peacock is." That is all.

King (to himself). His mother's name is Shakuntala! But names are alike. I trust this hope may not prove a disappointment in the end, like a mirage.

Boy. I like this little peacock, sister. Can it fly? (*He seizes the toy.*)

First woman (looks at the boy. Anxiously), Oh, the amulet is not on his wrist.

King. Do not be anxious, mother. It fell while he was struggling with the lion cub. (*He starts to pick it up.*)

The two women. Oh, don't, don't! (*They look at him.*) He has touched it! (*Astonished, they lay their hands on their bosoms, and look at each other.*)

King. Why did you try to prevent me?

First woman. Listen, your Majesty. This is a divine and most potent charm, called the Invincible. Marichi's holy son gave it to the baby when the birth-ceremony was performed. If it falls on the ground, no one may touch it except the boy's parents or the boy himself.

King. And if another touch it?

First woman. It becomes a serpent and stings him.

King. Did you ever see this happen to any one else?

Both women. More than once.

King (*joyfully*). Then why may I not welcome my hopes fulfilled at last? (*He embraces the boy.*)

Second woman. Come, Suvrata. Shakuntala is busy with her religious duties. We must go and tell her what has happened. (*Exeunt ambo.*)

Boy. Let me go. I want to see my mother.

King. My son, you shall go with me to greet your mother.

Boy. Dushyanta is my father, not you.

King (*smiling*). You show I am right by contradicting me. (*Enter* SHAKUNTALA, *wearing her hair in a single braid.*)

Shakuntala (*doubtfully*). I have heard that All-tamer's amulet did not change when it should have done so. But I do not trust my own happiness. Yet perhaps it is as Mishrakeshi told me. (*She walks about.*)

King (*looking at* SHAKUNTALA. *With plaintive joy*). It is she. It is Shakuntala.

The pale, worn face, the careless dress,
The single braid,
Show her still true, me pitiless,
The long vow paid.

Shakuntala (*seeing the king pale with remorse. Doubtfully*). It is not my husband. Who is the man that soils my boy with his caresses? The amulet should protect him. *Boy* (*running to his mother*). Mother, he is a man that belongs to other people. And he calls me his son.

King. My darling, the cruelty I showed you has turned to happiness. Will you not recognise me?

Shakuntala (*to herself*). Oh, my heart, believe it. Fate struck hard, but its envy is gone and pity takes its place. It is my husband.

King.

Black madness flies;
Comes memory;
Before my eyes
My love I see.

Eclipse flees far;
Light follows soon;
The loving star
Draws to the moon.

Shakuntala. Victory, victo---- (*Tears choke her utterance.*)

King.

The tears would choke you, sweet, in vain;
My soul with victory is fed,
Because I see your face again—
No jewels, but the lips are red.

Boy. Who is he, mother?

Shakuntala. Ask fate, my child. (*She weeps.*)

King.

Dear, graceful wife, forget;
Let the sin vanish;
Strangely did madness strive
Reason to banish.

Thus blindness works in men,
Love's joy to shake;
Spurning a garland, lest
It prove a snake. (*He falls at her feet.*)

Shakuntala. Rise, my dear husband. Surely, it was some old sin of mine that broke my happiness—though it has turned again to happiness. Otherwise, how could you, dear, have acted so? You are so kind. (*The king rises.*) But what brought back the memory of your suffering wife? *King*. I will tell you when I have plucked out the dart of sorrow.

'Twas madness, sweet, that could let slip
A tear to burden your dear lip;
On graceful lashes seen to-day,(*He does so.*)

Shakuntala (*sees more clearly and discovers the ring*). My husband, it is the ring!

King. Yes. And when a miracle recovered it, my memory returned.

Shakuntala. That was why it was so impossible for me to win your confidence.

King. Then let the vine receive her flower, as earnest of her union with spring.

Shakuntala. I do not trust it. I would rather you wore it.

(*Enter* MATALI)

Matali. I congratulate you, O King, on reunion with your wife and on seeing the face of your son.

King. My desires bear sweeter fruit because fulfilled through a friend. Matali, was not this matter known to Indra?

Matali (*smiling.*) What is hidden from the gods? Come. Marichi's holy son, Kashyapa, wishes to see you.

King. My dear wife, bring our son. I could not appear without you before the holy one.

Shakuntala. I am ashamed to go before such parents with my husband.

King. It is the custom in times of festival. Come. (*They walk about.* KASHYAPA *appears seated, with* ADITI.)

Kashyapa (*looking at the king*)..Aditi,

'Tis King Dushyanta, he who goes before
Your son in battle, and who rules the earth,

Whose bow makes Indra's weapon seem no more
Than a fine plaything, lacking sterner worth.

Aditi. His valour might be inferred from his appearance.

Matali. O King, the parents of the gods look upon you with a glance that betrays parental fondness. Approach them. *King.* Matali,

Sprung from the Creator's children, do I see
Great Kashyapa and Mother Aditi?
The pair that did produce the sun in heaven,
To which each year twelve changing forms are given;
That brought the king of all the gods to birth,
Who rules in heaven, in hell, and on the earth;
That Vishnu, than the Uncreated higher,
Chose as his parents with a fond desire.

Matali. It is indeed they.

King (*falling before them*). Dushyanta, servant of Indra, does reverence to you both.

Kashyapa. My son, rule the earth long.

Aditi. And be invincible. (SHAKUNTALA *and her son fall at their feet.*)

Kashyapa. My daughter,

Your husband equals Indra, king
Of gods; your son is like his son;
No further blessing need I bring:
Win bliss such as his wife has won.

Aditi. My child, keep the favour of your husband. And may this fine boy be an honour to the families of both parents. Come, let us be seated. (*All seat themselves.*)

Kashyapa (*indicating one after the other*).

Faithful Shakuntala, the boy,
And you, O King, I see
A trinity to bless the world—
Faith, Treasure, Piety.

King. Holy one, your favour shown to us is without parallel. You granted the fulfilment of our wishes before you called us to your presence. For, holy one,

The flower comes first, and then the fruit;
The clouds appear before the rain;
Effect comes after cause; but you
First helped, then made your favour plain.

Matali. O King, such is the favour shown by the parents of the world. *King*. Holy one, I married this your maid-servant by the voluntary ceremony. When after a time her relatives brought her to me, my memory failed and I rejected her. In so doing, I sinned against Kanva, who is kin to you. But afterwards, when I saw the ring, I perceived that I had married her. And this seems very wonderful to me.

Like one who doubts an elephant,
Though seeing him stride by,
And yet believes when he has seen
The footprints left; so I.

Kashyapa. My son, do not accuse yourself of sin. Your infatuation was inevitable. Listen.

King. I am all attention.

Kashyapa. When the nymph Menaka descended to earth and received Shakuntala, afflicted at her rejection, she came to Aditi. Then I perceived the matter by my divine insight. I saw that the unfortunate girl had been rejected by her rightful husband because of Durvasas' curse. And that the curse would end when the ring came to light.

King (*with a sigh of relief. To himself*). Then I am free from blame.

Shakuntala (*to herself*). Thank heaven! My husband did not reject me of his own accord. He really did not remember me. I suppose I did not hear the curse in my absent-minded state, for my friends warned me most earnestly to show my husband the ring.

Kashyapa. My daughter, you know the truth. Do not now give way to anger against your rightful husband. Remember:

The curse it was that brought defeat and pain;
The darkness flies; you are his queen again.
Reflections are not seen in dusty glass,
Which, cleaned, will mirror all the things that pass.

King. It is most true, holy one.

Kashyapa. My son, I hope you have greeted as he deserves the son whom Shakuntala has borne you, for whom I myself have performed the birth-rite and the other ceremonies.

King. Holy one, the hope of my race centres in him.

Kashyapa. Know then that his courage will make him emperor.

Journeying over every sea,
His car will travel easily;
The seven islands of the earth
Will bow before his matchless worth;
Because wild beasts to him were tame,
All-tamer was his common name;
As Bharata he shall be known,
For he will bear the world alone.

King. I anticipate everything from him, since you have performed the rites for him.

Aditi. Kanva also should be informed that his daughter's wishes are fulfilled. But Menaka is waiting upon me here and cannot be spared.

Shakuntala (*to herself*). The holy one has expressed my own desire.

Kashyapa. Kanva knows the whole matter through his divine insight. (*He reflects.*) Yet he should hear from us the pleasant tidings, how his daughter and her son have been received by her husband. Who waits without? (*Enter a pupil.*)

Pupil. I am here, holy one.

Kashyapa. Galava, fly through the air at once, carrying pleasant tidings from me to holy Kanva. Tell him how Durvasas' curse has come to an end, how Dushyanta recovered his memory, and has taken Shakuntala with her child to himself.

Pupil. Yes, holy one. (*Exit.*)

Kashyapa (*to the king*). My son, enter with child and wife the chariot of your friend Indra, and set out for your capital.

King. Yes, holy one.

Kashyapa. For now

May Indra send abundant rain,
Repaid by sacrificial gain;
With aid long mutually given,
Rule you on earth, and he in heaven.

King. Holy one, I will do my best.

Kashyapa. What more, my son, shall I do for you?

King. Can there be more than this? Yet may this prayer be fulfilled.

May kingship benefit the land,
And wisdom grow in scholars' band;
May Shiva see my faith on earth
And make me free of all rebirth.

(*Exeunt omnes.*